"Until this thing is over, you don't go anywhere without me..."

Caroline felt a chill wash over her. "You're scaring me, Jason."

To her surprise, he took her by the shoulders and turned her toward him, dipping his head to look directly into her eyes. "I'm not going to let anything happen to you, okay? As long as I'm with you, you're safe."

Before she could respond, he pulled her against him, enfolding her in his arms. Desire hit her like a sledgehammer, and she drew in a ragged breath, tightening her hold on him.

"Caroline..." His voice was a husky rasp against her ear.

Lifting her face, Caroline met his eyes. For just an instant, she saw the raw hunger in his eyes, and his expression gave her courage. Fixing her attention on his mouth, she told herself she would give him one kiss, just to thank him for everything he'd done. There was no harm in a simple gesture of gratitude, was there?

The kiss was so deep and so carnal, that Caroline's legs went a little weak, and she melted into him, welcoming the hot, slick slide of his tongue against hers.

As he bent her slightly back over his arm and feasted on the sensitive skin of her throat, Caroline forgot almost everything except the way he made her feel.

And in that moment, she realized that her life wasn't the only thing at risk.

D0838214

Blaze®

Dear Reader,

I've been intrigued by U.S. marshals ever since I first watched Timothy Olyphant portray badass deputy marshal Raylan Givens to smart, sexy perfection in the television series *Justified*.

While U.S. marshal Jason Cooper may not have grown up in the hardscrabble coal-mining community of Kentucky, his own upbringing was just as tough, and helped to forge his outlook on life—protect those you love at all costs. Even if they don't want your protection.

Caroline Banks has never forgotten—or forgiven—Jason's harsh rejection of her when she was just a teenager. But now that she's all grown up, she realizes her attraction to the sexy marshal is just as strong as ever. When someone targets her for murder, she knows that Jason is the one person who can keep her safe. But how is she going to resist him, especially when he seems determined to keep her close, day and night?

I hope you enjoy Jason and Caroline's story!

Happy reading!

Karen

Karen Foley

—

Make Me Melt

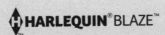

HARLEQUIN® BLAZE™

Recycling programs
for this product may
not exist in your area.

ISBN-13: 978-0-373-79801-8

MAKE ME MELT

Copyright © 2014 by Karen Foley

Printed In U.S.A.

ABOUT THE AUTHOR

Karen Foley is an incurable romantic. When she's not working for the Department of Defense, she's writing sexy romances with strong heroes and happy endings. She lives in Massachusetts with her husband and two daughters, an overgrown puppy, and two very spoiled cats. Karen enjoys hearing from her readers. You can find out more about her by visiting www.karenefoley.com.

Books by Karen Foley

HARLEQUIN BLAZE

*The U.S. Marshals

For Susan. Your courage and strength are an inspiration.

1

Twelve Years Earlier

ONE OF THE things that Caroline Banks liked best about Jason Cooper was that he was so different from any other guy she knew. He wasn't at all like the boys she went to high school with, or even like the Stanford University law students who frequently came over to the house to help her father handle his caseload, in the hopes of obtaining a judicial clerkship. Despite their ambitions and their wealthy families, they were all just boys.

Jason was unique.

Her dad, a superior court judge, apparently thought so, too. After Jason had made numerous appearances in his courtroom for various juvenile offenses, Judge William Banks had made an offer to the then sixteen-year-old: stay in school and get good grades, and he would help Jason attend college. The alternative was juvenile detention and—once he turned eighteen—the very real possibility of hard jail time. If he messed up even once, the offer would be withdrawn.

That had been five years ago, when Caroline had been just eleven years old. She still remembered the defiant, angry boy that Jason had been back then. At sixteen, he'd been taller than most boys his age, but he'd looked half-starved, and he'd sported visible scars on his face and body. But when she'd asked her father for details, he'd simply pinched her cheek and told her there were some things a little girl didn't need to know.

Now Caroline lay in the darkness of the guest bedroom and listened as the footsteps outside the room drew closer. She glanced at the bedside clock. Nearly one in the morning. She'd been battling her nerves for more than two hours, waiting for Jason to come upstairs and wondering if she'd have the nerve to remain in his room until he did. She'd had a crush on the reformed bad boy for as long as she could remember, and although he might act as if he didn't know she existed, Caroline knew better.

He'd just graduated from UCLA School of Law, and her father couldn't have been prouder than if Jason had been his own son. William had invited his protégé to stay with them at their beach house in Santa Cruz, in order to celebrate his success and discuss his future plans. Caroline hoped Jason would be blown away by how adult she looked; after all, she was now almost seventeen. That afternoon, she'd deliberately joined her father and Jason for lunch on the patio, wearing nothing but a string bikini. Her father had caught sight of her over his newspaper and scowled.

"What?" she'd demanded, widening her eyes. "I'm going to the beach right after I eat."

"Well, cover up until then." He'd glanced at Jason, whose eyes were resolutely focused on his plate, and snapped his newspaper in irritation. "Unlawful contact with a minor is still a punishable offense, even if it is provoked."

With a huff of annoyance, she'd returned to her room for a cover-up. When she'd come back to the table, Jason was gone.

"He's too old for you," her father had commented from behind his paper.

"Daddy," she'd grumbled in protest. "I'm not doing anything."

Her father had lowered his newspaper and removed his glasses. His blue eyes had been shrewd as he considered her. "It's times like this that I wish your mother was still alive," he'd finally said. "But she's not, so I'm going to say it like I see it. Jason Cooper is a fine young man, and I don't blame you for being attracted to him. But please stop tormenting him, and go practice your wiles on a boy your own age."

"Daddy."

He'd risen to his feet and stopped by her chair long enough to drop a kiss on top of her head and tweak a strand of her blond hair. "You're old enough to know exactly what you're doing to him and young enough to be forgiven for it. But he's just a man. Test him any further, and you may find the consequences more than you can handle. For his own sake, it's probably a good thing he's leaving tomorrow."

Now Caroline drew in a shaky breath and listened to Jason's approach. She knew she was doing the right thing. Her father had all but said Jason found her attractive. But he was leaving in the morning. She wasn't about to let him go without telling him how she felt.

The windows of the beach house were open, and the gauzy curtains billowed softly with the warm breeze that blew in from the Pacific, carrying with it the salt-tinged fragrance of the sea. In the distance, she could just hear the rhythmic pounding of the surf. Caroline curled her fingers around the sheet and waited. The pillowcase beneath her cheek smelled faintly of Jason—dark and woodsy. She breathed deeply, and the familiar scent lent her some courage.

When the door finally opened, she saw him silhouetted briefly in the hallway before he stepped inside and drew it closed behind him. Caroline's heart beat so hard and fast in her chest that for a moment, she wondered if he might hear it. In the dim light of the room, he didn't see her lying quiet and still in the bed, but her eyes were accustomed to the darkness, and she could see him clearly.

He walked past the foot of the bed toward the open windows, unbuttoning his shirt as he went. He finally peeled it off and dropped it onto the back of a nearby chair. He stood at the windows. Pale moonlight slanted in through the open casement, illuminating his body and revealing the strong slope of his shoulders and the muscled definition of his arms. Her eyes widened as she caught sight of the tattoos on his shoulders and across his back. She couldn't make them out clearly, but the black ink was unmistakable against his skin. She'd known he had them—had caught sight of them once as a young girl when he'd taken a late afternoon swim in their pool. But when he'd realized she was watching him from her playhouse in the corner of the yard, he'd quickly pulled himself out of the water and dragged a shirt over his head. She'd never seen the tattoos again, and she wondered if he deliberately kept them covered because he was ashamed of them.

He braced his hands on the sill and leaned forward, letting his head drop, as if torn by some inner conflict. He stood like that for a long moment before straightening and scrubbing a hand over his hair.

Toeing his shoes off, he shucked his jeans and walked toward the bed. Caroline knew the precise instant that he became aware of her presence. He reached for the sheet that covered her and then recoiled.

"Jesus." His voice was a shocked rasp, scraping across her senses like rough velvet.

Terrified that he might leave, Caroline surged to her knees on the bed, hands reaching for him as the sheet fell away. "Please don't go. I need to tell you something."

He caught her wrists when she would have touched him, but he didn't thrust her away, as she'd half expected. Emboldened, she leaned toward him. He wore a pair of boxer briefs and nothing else, and she could smell the scent of his skin. As always, it turned her thoughts to dark, forbidden acts. She had zero experience in that department, but her imagination was rampant with images of how it would be with him.

"Caroline, you shouldn't be in here." His voice was low, tense.

"I had to. You're leaving tomorrow." She scooted closer on her knees, until she was at the very edge of the mattress. "I wanted to tell you that I—I love you. And I want you to be my first."

In the stunned silence that followed her declaration, Caroline could hear the whooshing of her own blood in her ears.

"No." He pushed her hands away and took a jerky step back. "You don't. Jesus, you're just a kid."

"I'm not. I'm almost seventeen. All my friends have already lost their virginity." She stepped off the bed and, before he could retreat, pressed her body against his. When she slid her arms around his lean waist, he went rigid in her embrace. "Please, Jason," she entreated, smoothing her hands over his skin. "You're all I think about."

He grasped her shoulders and tried to shove her away. His voice sounded strangled. "Are you naked?"

"Not yet. I'm still wearing panties."

"You need to go back to your own room. What if your father comes in?"

"He won't," she assured him. "He never comes up-stairs."

William's bedroom was located on the first floor, at the farthest end of the beach house. He typically went to bed in the wee hours of the morning, but once asleep, Caroline knew that very little would wake him up.

"I can't stop thinking about you," she continued. "Please kiss me."

His eyes, the exact shade of tempered glass, glinted

in the indistinct light, and she shivered at the heat she saw reflected there.

"Caroline—"

"Please, Jason." She raised herself on tiptoe and pressed gentle kisses against his collarbone, his throat and anywhere she could reach. He tried to hold himself rigidly away, but Caroline pressed herself against him until her breasts were flattened between them. She let her hands stroke over his back and lower. When she smoothed her palms over the firm mounds of his buttocks and raised her hips to his, he gave a harsh groan, and she felt his restraint give way like the moorings of a storm-tossed ship.

"Caroline."

The word came out like a plea, and she felt her heart leap. Then he thrust his hands into her hair and bent his head to cover her mouth with his own; his taste surrounded her. She'd been kissed before, but never like this. He swept his tongue past her lips, stroking the inside of her mouth until heat blasted through every cell in her body, and she felt boneless with pleasure. She drew in a shuddering breath when he released her mouth and dragged his lips along the side of her throat.

"So sweet," he muttered against her skin. "So soft and so damned sweet."

When he cupped one bare breast in his hand, Caroline gasped. He caressed her gently, kneading and rolling her nipple in his fingers. "Oh, my God," she breathed. "That feels so good."

Nobody had ever touched her so intimately, and she had no idea that her breasts could be so sensitive, tightening beneath his touch and sending a jolt of sensation to her groin, where moisture simmered.

When Jason dipped his head and drew her nipple into his mouth, the feeling was so intense that Caroline clutched at his shoulders and gave a helpless moan. Beneath her palms, his body was sleek with muscle and his skin radiated heat. He laved her with his tongue, while he squeezed and fondled her other breast.

She closed her eyes, swamped with sensation, her body restless. This was finally happening, and the reality of it exceeded all her fantasies. How long had she dreamed of this? Each time he came to visit her father, especially over the past year, her yearning for him grew, until there was only him. She hadn't been sure he would want her—he was always so distant with her. Maybe this didn't mean anything to him beyond a momentary physical release, but right now she didn't care. The way he made her feel—she couldn't stop even if she wanted to.

And she definitely didn't want to.

And now that she'd had a taste of him, she didn't think she could ever be happy with anyone else. With Jason, there was no awkward groping or wet kisses. Everything he did was done with confidence. Even at twenty-one, he was no stranger to sensual pleasure.

She was unprepared when he lifted her in his arms and laid her down on the bed, following her with the length of his body. He braced himself on one elbow while he continued to nuzzle her breast, and one thigh insinuated itself between hers.

"Yes," she breathed and instinctively raised her hips to rub herself against him. The contact sent a flood of moisture to her center. She could feel him, hard and hot, against her stomach, and the knowledge that he was aroused caused her pulse to quicken until she could feel the need for him throb through every vein in her body, all the way to her fingertips.

He kissed her again, deeper this time, and slid his hand over her stomach to the waistband of her panties. But instead of slipping his fingers inside, he cupped her through the fragile material. Caroline widened her legs to give him better access.

"Yes," she whispered against his lips. "Touch me."

Jason made a groaning sound and eased the elastic aside. Then his fingers were there, skimming over her sensitized flesh and parting her folds.

"Jesus," he said, his breath harsh against her cheek. "You're so slippery."

Caroline made a sobbing sound, desperate for him to touch her there, where she craved it the most. When his fingers swirled her slickness over her quivering flesh, she gave a soft cry, and her hips jerked reflexively. Then he eased one finger inside her, and Caroline felt her muscles contract around him. The sensation was unlike anything she could have imagined. She felt stretched and tight, aching for something just beyond her reach. Desperate, she clutched at his shoulders, mindless with need. She needed… She needed so much, and she was so afraid that if she didn't take this now, she might never have another chance. When he began moving his finger, she arched into his palm.

"Oh, my God," she panted. "That feels so amazing. I want you inside me."

His hand stilled.

When he drew it away, Caroline thought he meant to pull her panties off, and she reached down to help him. Instead, he carefully disentangled himself from her limbs. Standing up, he scrubbed both hands over his face.

"Get dressed." His voice was low and harsh.

Still throbbing and unfulfilled, Caroline was too bewildered to do more than lie there. He turned to look at her. Even in the darkness, she felt his eyes on her, as palpable as a physical touch. With his dark hair and glittering eyes, and the tattoos that snaked over his shoulders, he looked a little like a pirate. Caroline shivered.

"Jason…what's wrong?"

"All of this. I'm not the right guy for you, Caroline, and you don't want this. Not with me."

She sat up. "I do! I want you to be my first."

"You have no idea what you want, and if your father ever knew about this, he'd kill me. Or have me thrown in jail."

"No!" Caroline rose to her feet, but when she would have touched him, he warded her off. "I won't tell anyone," she promised. "I'd never do that."

"I. Can't. Do. This." He bit the words out between gritted teeth. "Don't you get it? You're sixteen! I'm twenty-one."

"I don't care," she cried, reaching for him. "I'm old enough! This is what I want."

He put out an arm to hold her off. "That's the problem. You always get what you want, even if it's not good for you. You're spoiled and selfish, and you never think about anyone but yourself. But not this time. I'm not going to let you ruin my life." He looked around the room, finally scooping up a bathrobe from the floor beside the bed. He thrust it toward her. "Get dressed. Go back to your room, and forget this ever happened. It was a mistake."

Caroline hugged the robe against her breasts, and her breath hitched with a suppressed sob. She couldn't believe he was being so cruel. Maybe her father did spoil her, but that wasn't her fault. But selfish? Nobody had ever accused her of that before. "Please," she begged. "If you'd just give us a chance… I love you."

He closed his eyes for a moment, and when he opened them again, Caroline saw his resolve.

"Well, I don't love you. Trust me—you'll thank me one day," he said. He strode to the window and braced his hands on the sill, not looking at her. "Now get out of here."

She stood looking at his bowed shoulders, her tears blurring his image. He had wanted her. She hadn't been mistaken about that. But his rejection felt as if he'd just ripped her beating heart out of her chest. She'd never known such agonizing pain. And as much as she loved him, she wanted to hurt him, too. To make him feel just a little bit of what she was feeling right now.

"I won't be sixteen forever," she finally managed, hating how her voice shook. "Someday I'll be a woman. But it will be too late for you. By the time your conscience decides I'm old enough, I'll have had a dozen other guys. You only get one chance to be someone's first, Jason."

He spun around, and whatever triumph she might have felt dissolved beneath the stark bleakness of his expression.

"I'm doing this for your own good. And because I have too much respect for your father to take advantage of you. I owe him more than that."

Caroline pulled her robe on with jerky movements and yanked the belt tight around her waist with trembling fingers. If she stayed another second, she would begin to cry, and there was no way she wanted him to witness that. She raised her chin, taking refuge in lashing out at him. "Whatever. I guess the other guys were right about you, after all. Do you know what my father's law students say about you?"

He remained silent.

"They say you're gutter trash," she continued in a rush, even though she didn't believe that about him for a second. "They say a leopard can't change its spots, and I guess it's true. Is that why you hide your tattoos? Because you know, deep down, that if people see them, they'll know the truth about you? About what you really are?"

When he didn't answer, Caroline felt small and mean. Being cruel wasn't in her nature. People always said she was like her mother—sweet and kind. But right now, a part of her wanted to wound Jason. Another part of her wanted to fling herself against his chest and tell him she didn't mean any of what she'd just said. But she wouldn't risk him rejecting her yet again.

"I won't wait for you, just so you know."

Caroline stood uncertainly for a moment, hoping against hope that he might say something to stop her from leaving.

"No," he finally said, and his voice sounded weary.

"I wouldn't expect you to wait and I don't want you to. Just leave."

With a muffled sob, she fled.

2

Present Day

CAROLINE STUFFED HER files into her leather carry case, snapped it shut and glanced at her watch. It was nearly ten o'clock, and she'd told the social services caseworker, Patrick Dougherty, that she would stop by the child welfare office as soon as possible to discuss Devon Lawton's case. The boy had run away from home—again. The police had caught him breaking into a convenience store early that morning and had arrested him. Devon had borne the evidence of a vicious beating, and although he'd refused to name the person responsible, Caroline suspected it was his father.

Now the police wanted to put Devon into juvenile detention, while Caroline knew what he really needed was a safe, stable home environment. But at fourteen, he already had a growing rap sheet, and she seriously doubted that they'd be able to find a suitable foster family willing to take him in. He was a smart kid, and she believed with the right support, he could turn his life around. Both of his parents were alcoholics, and she suspected they did drugs, as well. Each time he got into trouble, the courts returned him to his family. There had never been any evidence of physical abuse...until now. Caroline hadn't seen Devon yet, but Patrick had told her the boy was a mess.

She stopped by her boss's office on her way out of the impressive marble building in downtown Richmond, Virginia, that housed the law firm of MacInness, Shively and Crane. Arthur MacInness, one of the senior partners, was standing behind his gleaming desk, studying a document he held in his hands. Through the towering bank of windows behind him, Caroline had a perfect vantage point of the entire city. Storm clouds had gathered overhead, and the skies looked sullen and dark. Arthur glanced up as she knocked softly on his open door. He lowered his glasses in a way that reminded Caroline of her father.

"I'm heading over to the child welfare office," she said. "One of my kids pulled a B and E overnight, but it sounds like he was beaten black-and-blue beforehand, probably by his father. I'll be back in the morning."

He nodded. "Very well. Just don't let your pro bono work interfere with your other cases here."

After she'd passed the bar exam, and been hired at MacInness, Shively and Crane as a junior attorney, Caroline had found the work exciting and challenging. But after nearly two years of working on behalf of wealthy couples battling for child custody, she had started to feel unfulfilled. It wasn't until she'd begun volunteering her legal services in support of the city's underprivileged citizens that she'd felt infinitely more satisfied. And when she'd begun to focus those efforts on the youngest citizens—the children—she knew she'd finally found her calling.

She would have preferred that work exclusively, but she had bills to pay. So she'd hammered out a deal with her firm to devote a portion of her time to pro bono work through the child welfare office. The work indirectly benefited the firm, as the effort made them look at least somewhat philanthropic.

Last week, the district attorney's office had offered her a full-time position on its staff, based on the pro bono work she'd done. She'd be a child advocate, representing children who otherwise would have nobody to speak up for them. She was considering the offer, although it would mean a cut in pay from what she was currently making. It would also mean she'd be able to work full-time on behalf of the city's needy children. The work appealed to her. In fact, it was exactly the kind of work she'd hoped to do full-time. So what was holding her back from accepting the job? She wanted to make a difference in the lives of troubled kids, but she just wasn't sure whether she wanted to do it here in Richmond.

Lately she'd found her thoughts turning more and more frequently toward San Francisco. She'd told herself a million times that it had nothing to do with Jason Cooper, or the notion that he'd once been a kid just like Devon. She was just missing her father. On some level, the work she did made her feel closer to him…and she'd been thinking that maybe it was time she went home, this time for good.

After she'd graduated from law school, she'd moved

permanently to the East Coast, determined to get a job on her own terms, without her father's influence. At the time, he'd still been a superior court judge, and he had connections with most of the bigger law firms in the area. It wouldn't matter if Caroline was hired strictly on her own merit; she knew there'd be people who would always say her father had helped her out. So she'd gone to the opposite side of the country, where few people had ever heard of William Banks.

She liked Richmond, but it wasn't home. Besides, her father wasn't getting any younger. He'd also been appointed to the Supreme Court of California several years ago, and Caroline worried about the toll his job was having on his health. But maybe they could escape to the beach house in Santa Cruz for a weekend. It would be just like old times.

Well, almost, she amended silently.

He wouldn't be there.

She knew that Jason still kept in touch with her father and frequently made the seven-hour trip from San Diego to San Francisco to spend time with Judge Banks. Somehow, even with the demands of being a U.S. marshal, Jason managed to spend more time with her father than she did. No question about it—she was a terrible daughter.

But Jason was precisely the reason Caroline avoided going home. She'd seen him just once since that disastrous night when she'd practically begged him to have sex with her. She had just graduated college and had been accepted into law school on the East Coast. Her father had made a big deal out of the event, throwing her a party at the beach house. Jason had been there, and although she'd been acutely aware of him watching her, he hadn't spoken to her and had left before she could gather enough courage to approach him. As a deputy marshal, he'd been even sexier than she remembered, and her heart had leaped at the sight of him.

She'd wanted him to see her as a grown woman, and there'd been no shortage of cute guys at the party to flirt with. She'd done her best to make sure that Jason knew she could have any one of them. But he'd apparently been less than impressed. When he'd taken off without uttering a single word to her, she'd felt sixteen years old all over again. After he was gone, the party had been over for her.

That had been seven years ago. While she was definitely over Jason Cooper, she had no desire to have him drop in unexpectedly while she was visiting her father. As a result, she rarely visited, preferring to have her dad come out and stay with her in Virginia. Because he had friends in Washington, he usually conceded to her requests, but she knew she couldn't continue to expect him to travel across the country every time he wanted to see her.

Hefting her carry bag over her shoulder, she took the elevator to the first floor of the building and made her way across the spacious lobby, the heels of her shoes echoing on the polished marble. The first floor was only moderately busy at this time of day, with a few stragglers returning from lunch, laughing and shaking moisture from their hair and shoulders as they entered the building. Through the glass doors that led to the street, Caroline saw it had begun to rain. Pausing, she slid her bag around to where she could unzip the outer compartment and pulled out her umbrella.

When she looked up again, two men were pushing through the rotating doors. Caroline's breath caught, and her feet remained glued to the floor.

The first man wore khaki fatigues, a dark blue polo shirt and a matching baseball cap. He had the distinctive bearing of a law enforcement officer. If the weapon in his hip holster didn't grab your attention, the U.S. Marshals logo emblazoned on the breast of his shirt did.

But it was the second man who caused Caroline's heart to skip a beat and almost stutter to a stop before exploding into frenzied overdrive.

Jason Cooper.

He wore a black sports jacket and shirt, paired with well-worn blue jeans and boots. He had an easy, loose-limbed stride that Caroline would have recognized anywhere. As he made his way across the lobby toward her, she caught a glimpse of the badge he wore on his belt— the silver star of a U.S. marshal.

The years had done nothing to diminish his good looks or the vague aura of danger that clung to him. He was bigger than she remembered, having lost the lean gauntness of his youth. Beneath the jacket, she could see his shoulders and chest were thick with muscle. He looked as if he kicked ass for a living.

His dark hair was cut short, and his skin was burnished from the sun. But it was his eyes that held her riveted. They still reminded her of tempered glass, and right now they were fixed on her with unsettling intensity. His square jaw was set in grim lines. As he met her gaze, frissons of dread fingered their way along her spine.

Raising her chin, she looked directly at Jason and forced herself to speak with a calm that she was far from feeling. Her fingers closed convulsively around the umbrella in her hands. "Marshal Cooper. You're a long way from home."

Caroline tried to quell the erratic rhythm of her heart. Fear caused her stomach to roll, and for a moment she was afraid she might actually be sick. She knew there could be only one reason he had flown all the way to Virginia to seek her out at work.

"Caroline." He indicated the officer beside him. "This is Deputy Marshal Colton Black."

His voice hadn't changed at all, and the sound of it, low and a little rough around the edges, brought a tidal wave of memories flooding back. It seemed some things never changed, because the quality of his voice still had the ability to make her shiver. But all those years ago, his voice had been husky with arousal and then harsh with rejection; now he was all business. He regarded her as if she were a stranger.

Two women walked past them toward the elevators, giving both Jason and his deputy appreciative smiles. Caroline recognized them from the real estate division of the law firm, and she fervently hoped they wouldn't decide to stop and strike up a conversation to get a better look at the marshals.

"Is there somewhere private we can talk?" Jason asked, eyeing the women.

She gave a jerky nod and indicated a semiprivate sitting area on the far side of the lobby. Jason took her elbow to guide her. The touch of his fingers seemed to burn through her suit jacket to the sensitive skin of her inner arm, and she had to suppress the instinctive urge to pull away. As if sensing her discomfort, he let his hand drop, indicating she should precede him toward the cozy arrangement of upholstered chairs and sofas. His deputy moved to the far side of the lobby and directed his gaze through the windows to where the rain sleeted against the glass. For the first time in years, Caroline found herself alone with Jason.

Setting her bag down, she perched on the edge of the sofa. She was surprised when he sat down beside her. Drawing a fortifying breath, she turned to him, dread and anxiety twisting her stomach into tight ribbons. "Just tell me. He's dead, isn't he? Why else would you be here?"

He closed his eyes for a moment, and when he opened them again, she saw something in his light green eyes that might have been pain. Then his expression grew shuttered, and he shook his head. "No, your father's alive, but just barely."

Relief swamped Caroline, so strong that for a moment, she went weak and covered her face with her hands. Immediately, Jason put an arm around her shoulders and gathered her close, lending her his strength. She allowed herself to lean into him, if only briefly. He smelled exactly as she remembered, like something woodsy and dark, and she had to resist the urge to burrow her face into his chest. Instead, she pulled away and dragged air into her lungs.

"What happened?"

Jason considered her, as if assessing whether or not she was strong enough to hear what he was about to say. His eyes were so bleak that for an instant, Caroline wasn't sure she wanted to hear.

"He was shot while answering his front door last night. I'm sorry."

Caroline closed her eyes briefly as her chest constricted painfully. Whatever she'd expected him to say, it hadn't been that. She'd imagined him having a heart attack, either at home or at his office. But to be shot on his own front steps... The image that sprang to mind was so graphic she had to push it away.

Her father had spent his life giving to others and striving to make the world a better place. Jason Cooper was living proof of William Banks's goodness and generosity. But Caroline also knew that as a Supreme Court judge, his rulings on controversial issues had likely gained him enemies. Still, when she thought of his bright blue eyes, full of shrewdness and humor, she couldn't imagine that anyone would hate him enough to attack him in his own home. She recalled him always being so full of life and so active. When she was growing up, there'd hardly ever been a day when they didn't have visitors or when her father wasn't meeting someone for lunch or dinner. The knowledge that he was now fighting for his life left her feeling dazed. He was all she had left, and she didn't know what she would do if she lost him. He'd been both mother and father to her, had been there for every important event in her life. He'd gone prom dress shopping with her, had hosted more slumber parties than she could recall and had sat up late with her on countless Saturday nights, watching romantic comedies and eating ice cream. He was everything to her, and the thought that she might lose him made her feel sick with both guilt and grief.

"Who would do such a thing?" She swiped a hand across her eyes. "And why?"

"We'll find the person who did this," Jason assured her. "We already have a team working it."

"We have to go. Now." She rose quickly, feeling a little panicky. "I need to book a flight. He'll need me there with him."

"Already done," Jason said, standing also. "We depart from Richmond airport in two hours. Do you need to go home and pack anything?"

"Yes." Her mind whirled with all the things she should do before she left, but there was no time. She needed to get to her father's side. She could make some calls on the way to the airport. She'd talk to Patrick Dougherty and recommend another attorney for Devon Lawton. Then she'd call Arthur MacInness, and explain what had happened and let him know she'd likely be gone for several weeks. The rest would have to wait until she reached San Francisco.

"I'll drive you to your house, and then we'll head to the airport."

"Thank you." She swallowed. "Did you— Have you seen him?"

Jason shook his head. "No. I got the news just before midnight. An hour later, Deputy Marshal Black and I were on the red-eye from San Diego."

Caroline could hardly believe her ears. "Why?" she asked. "Why would you come straight here, when you could have gone to San Francisco to be at my father's bedside?" A small part of her—the part that still held on to girlish fantasies—wondered if he might have come directly to her because, on some level, he did care for her. But in the next instant, those childish thoughts were banished.

"Caroline," he said patiently, as if she really were no more than a child, "the U.S. Marshals Service is charged with providing protection for federal judges."

"Yes, I understand. But my father is a judge in San Francisco, and your district is San Diego. Are you saying that you've been assigned to protect him?"

He gave her a humorless smile. "No. I'm here to protect you."

She stared at him, uncomprehending. "Me? But why?"

"Until the assailant is captured, we have to assume the judge's life is still in danger. It's standard protocol to assign a protection detail to immediate family members, as well."

She shook her head, unwilling to accept what he was telling her. She didn't want Jason to protect her. The news of her father had left her feeling vulnerable and emotionally ragged. She didn't want Jason to see her like this. Having him witness her fear and grief was far too intimate.

"But why you? This is out of your jurisdiction. Why wouldn't you assign a marshal from the San Francisco district to protect me?" She couldn't keep the strain out of her voice. "Why does it have to be you?"

Jason's expression darkened. "Because despite the fact you clearly don't give a shit about your old man, you're the single most important person in his life," he said, his voice hard. "Call it a professional courtesy. I'm doing this for him, not for you. I owe him that, at least."

JASON GLANCED AT the woman who sat beside him in the car, tense and unhappy. She'd hardly spoken during the long flight from Virginia to San Francisco. Not that he blamed her. He hadn't been overly sympathetic to her.

Even his deputy had given him a look that would have withered most other men. But he and Colton had worked together for more than five years, and the other man was as close to a friend as he'd probably ever have. He glanced into his rearview mirror, noting the unmarked car that carried Colton and another deputy. Between the three of them, they would provide around-the-clock security to ensure Caroline's safety.

The Caroline Banks he'd once known had changed. Gone was the sweetly passionate teenager who'd worn her heart on her sleeve. In her place was a coolly assured woman whose brittle demeanor and aloofness he hardly recognized. If his own manner toward her had been on the cool side, it was because she'd made so little effort to come home to visit her father. She'd been home once in the past five years. Judge Banks never complained, but Jason knew it hurt him. Caroline was his only child. While Jason loved the judge like a father, they weren't family. His own frequent trips to San Francisco couldn't make up for the fact that his daughter never came to visit.

Physically, she'd changed, too.

Her blond hair was darker than he remembered, layered with wheaten and caramel strands, and her normally tanned skin was pale, as if she hadn't seen the sun in years. Yeah, she'd really put the California girl behind her when she'd cut out for the East Coast. Whenever he thought about Caroline—which was far too often, considering how much time had passed since he'd last seen her—she was always wearing a bikini or some skimpy outfit that showed way too much skin. The woman sitting next to him wore a pantsuit that had probably cost more than his monthly rent. She was so buttoned-up and conservative that he had a difficult time reconciling her with the exuberant girl of his memories.

But one thing hadn't changed. His reaction to her had been immediate and so powerful that he'd had to draw on all his professional training to keep his emotions concealed. For just an instant, when she'd looked up at him in the lobby and their gazes had collided, he'd seen shock, then something that looked like hunger, in her eyes before she'd swiftly schooled her expression.

He'd been unprepared for how time and maturity had refined her beauty, sculpting her features and softening her curves. Caroline Banks had been an exceptionally pretty teenager. Now she was a drop-dead gorgeous woman, and the first thought that had steamrolled through his mind was that he'd completely blown it all those years ago when she'd asked him to be her first.

Realistically, he knew he'd done the right thing turning her away, but the knowledge that she'd likely had numerous lovers in the ensuing years bugged the hell out of him. Clenching his jaw, he told himself again— as he'd done a hundred times since—that he'd had no other choice.

Now he glanced at her as they parked near a rear entrance of the hospital, where several California state troopers stood near the doors. Her eyes widened, and she turned to look at him.

"Are they here for my father?"

"Until we catch the perpetrator, they'll provide twenty-four-hour protection."

"Why? Do you think whoever shot him will want to finish the job?"

Jason heard the underlying anxiety in her voice.

"That isn't going to happen. We have our best men standing guard outside his room."

He'd give his own life before he let anything happen to Judge Banks.

Or to Caroline.

"Thanks," she said, nodding stiffly.

"Are you ready?"

She drew in a deep breath. "Yes. I think so."

But moments later, standing by her father's bedside, Jason knew she hadn't been prepared for the sight of William Banks lying still and unresponsive, attached to a dozen monitors and tubes. Even Jason, who had seen numerous victims, found it unsettling.

Without the sparkle of his blue eyes or the energy of his personality in evidence, the judge looked old and frail. His mouth was slack, and his silver hair was in disarray. Above the thick bandage on his chest, his skin was stained orange from the surgical antiseptic. Jason noted traces of blood remained on his neck and jaw from the splatter of where he had been shot. Anger swirled through him, building and gathering like a dark storm. They'd find the person responsible, and he'd make sure they paid for what they had done to William. For what they had done to Caroline. For what they had done to him.

CAROLINE SAT BY her father's bedside for the next several hours. At first, she'd just wept silently, but then she'd composed herself and covered his hand with her own, talking to him in soothing tones, despite the fact he was in a deep coma. She'd removed her jacket, revealing a white blouse that was so sheer, Jason could see the lacy outline of her bra beneath it. Her blond hair had begun to come loose from the clip she used to hold it back, and he liked how the tumbling locks made her look less aloof. If he'd had any doubts that she loved her father, it was dispelled by the expression he saw on her face as she held his hand.

Finally, she leaned forward and pressed a lingering kiss against his forehead before rising to her feet. She glanced at Jason, then turned away and swiftly swiped her fingers across her cheeks. She picked up her jacket from where she had draped it across the arm of her chair and pivoted to face him. Jason was relieved to see she'd dried her tears. When she cried, he had an almost irresistible urge to drag her into his arms and comfort her.

"So what now?" she asked quietly. "The doctor said the next forty-eight hours are critical."

She wanted him to reassure her that the judge would pull through, that he'd make a full recovery. But Jason couldn't do that. He'd read the medical report. William had lost a tremendous amount of blood and had been in full cardiac arrest when they'd brought him into the emergency room. His injuries were so grave that the doctors had put him into a medically induced coma. He'd suffered brain damage, but they wouldn't know the full extent of impairment until he regained consciousness.

If he regained consciousness.

Jason didn't want to think about that. Everything he had—his education, his career and even his outlook on life—he owed to the judge. Losing him would be worse than losing his own father. And if he felt that way, he could only imagine what Caroline was going through. Seeing how hard she tried to camouflage her emotions and put on a good face made him feel a surge of sympathy for her.

"You know, it's okay to cry," he said. "You don't need to hide your feelings from me."

She gave a disbelieving laugh. "Oh, yes, I do. I absolutely do."

Before Jason could respond, a nurse walked into the room and began to change the judge's IV drip.

"Stay here as long you'd like," he urged Caroline. "I'll wait outside in the hallway."

She hesitated. "Would you like to spend some time alone with him? After all, he's as much your father as he is mine."

For just a moment, Jason was too surprised by her perceptiveness to respond. He hadn't been the only troubled youth who'd benefited from the judge's generosity, but he knew he was one of the few who'd maintained a close relationship with him over the years. While others had used their friendship with her father to advance their own careers, Jason had genuinely loved the older man and had enjoyed spending time with him. Even after he'd joined the U.S. Marshals Service, and his future had been secure, that hadn't changed. But he wasn't going to do Judge Banks any good by standing vigil at his bedside. Not when the person responsible was still out there, maybe hoping to finish the job.

"Thanks," he said, "but if you're ready to go, then so am I. The best way I can serve your father is to protect you."

For a moment, she looked taken aback. "You're serious. You think my life is in danger."

"I have to make that assumption." He gestured toward the bed. "But you can stay with him for as long as you'd like. I'm not going anywhere."

She shook her head "No, that's okay. It's getting late, and he doesn't even know I'm here. I'll come back in the morning. I think I'd just like to go home."

Jason knew she meant the house in Sea Cliff, where she had grown up. "I'm afraid that's not possible," he told her. "The house is an active crime scene, and the investigators are still gathering possible clues."

"Oh." Her brows knitted together as she considered this. "Okay. Then I'll find a hotel."

"I already booked a suite of rooms for us at the Fairmont. It's close to the hospital, and the security there is excellent."

Jason saw something like panic flash in her eyes. "Us?" she repeated.

"Until this thing is over, I'm your personal protection detail," he reminded her. "Where you go, I go."

"Like a bodyguard? Is that really necessary?" Caroline

clenched her hands at her sides, and her voice sounded a little desperate. "You said yourself that the security at the hotel is excellent. It's my father who needs the protection, not me. Why can't you just stay here, with him?"

"Not an option," he said grimly. "There are two men standing guard outside the room and two more downstairs. Your father is secure—my job is to ensure your safety. If you're ready to go, we'll leave."

"Oh, my God, this is crazy," she muttered and rubbed a hand over the back of her neck. The movement caused her blouse to stretch tautly across her breasts, and Jason tried not to notice the faintest shadow of her nipples beneath the lacy fabric of her bra. After a moment, she sighed. "Okay, fine. I'll stay in a hotel if you insist, but I'd like to stop by the house first. I want to see where my father was shot."

Jason hesitated. He was sworn to protect her at all costs. And not just from physical danger. Seeing her father fighting for his life in a hospital was bad enough. Witnessing the evidence of the violence that had sent him there, splattered across her front porch, was another thing altogether. He didn't want her exposed to that kind of ugliness.

"I don't think that's a good idea."

He watched as her eyes narrowed and she tipped her chin up in a gesture that he remembered too well. "I'm not a child anymore, Jason."

He hadn't even seen the crime scene, although he had a good idea of what to expect. But she had been sheltered and pampered her entire life. Neither her expensive education nor her law degree would have prepared her for the rawness of what he suspected awaited her at her father's house. But he was beginning to understand that she was right—she was no longer a child, and there were some things even he couldn't protect her from.

"Fine," he said in a clipped tone. "Let's go."

With a satisfied nod, she pushed past him and strode into the hallway, leaving him with no choice but to follow her. Just outside the hospital room, he paused to withdraw a small surveillance earpiece from his pocket and insert it, ensuring communication with the rest of his team. As he adjusted the earpiece, he didn't miss how the two guards sitting outside the hospital room followed Caroline's progress with their eyes. Not that he blamed them. She was a beautiful woman, and her hips swung enticingly with each determined stride. She'd taken about ten steps when she stopped and turned.

"Are you coming?" she demanded. "How are you going to protect me if you can't even keep up with me?"

Without waiting for a reply, she continued toward the exit. Jason exchanged a knowing look with the two guards before following her. As he reached her side, he acknowledged soberly that while he could protect Caroline from whatever dangers might lie in wait outside the hospital, he wasn't sure he could protect her from himself.

3

As THE CAR drew up in front of her father's house, Caroline could feel Jason's eyes on her. She knew that he was unhappy with her request to view the crime scene. She couldn't explain to him her need to see where the horrific event had happened, to be able to visualize what had occurred when her father had answered the door. She hoped, too, that maybe she could help the investigators. Perhaps she would see something they had overlooked.

But whatever she had expected to see, it wasn't the police cruisers and unmarked vehicles parked in front of the house and in the driveway. Several news vans were parked along the street, and it was only the quick action of the police that kept the reporters from mobbing their car as they pulled up to the curb.

Although it was just past six o'clock, it was still light outside, and Caroline could see the yellow police tape that surrounded the residence.

The sight of so many law enforcement personnel seemed incongruous, given the affluent neighborhood of mansions and meticulously manicured lawns. Crime in this area was virtually unheard of, and Caroline couldn't believe anyone would have the nerve to commit such a heinous act in full view of the street, the neighbors and anyone else who might be watching. Of course, it had been close to midnight when the crime had occurred, so the likelihood of any witnesses was slim to none. Her father had always preferred to stay up until the wee hours of the morning.

"Maybe it was just a random act. He liked to stay up late, so maybe someone saw his light on and just chose him arbitrarily."

She didn't realize she'd said the words aloud until Jason thrust the car into Park and turned toward her.

"Everything indicates he was targeted."

"But why? He's a good man—the best. Why would anyone want to hurt him?"

He didn't answer, shifting his attention toward the house. "Are you sure you want to do this?"

Caroline followed his gaze to where several officers stood near the wide front porch, watching them. She recognized Deputy Black, who had followed them to the house in a separate car. Unlike the other men, he stood vigil near the sidewalk and scanned the surrounding area as if on alert for any unseen threat.

"I need to do this," she finally answered, reaching for the door handle.

As she approached the porch, she was conscious of Jason's protective bulk close by her side. The other officers stood back and allowed them to pass. Caroline climbed the steps slowly, aware that her heart was thudding hard in her chest. The front door was open, and she could see two more men standing inside the house. Nothing could have prepared her for the sight of the blood.

The dark stain spread across the hardwood floor just inside the entryway and seeped into the edge of the Persian-style carpet. She had a sudden, vivid image of her father opening the door, only to be greeted by an explosive bullet to the chest. She envisioned him staggering back into the hallway and collapsing onto the floor as his assailant stood over him. The picture was so real, and so frightening, that for an instant, she couldn't breathe. She heard a roaring in her ears, and black wings fluttered at the edge of her vision. She was only vaguely aware of strong arms coming around her as the floor rose up to meet her.

"Put your head down and take some deep breaths."

Even if Caroline had wanted to refuse, Jason's hand was at the back of her neck, large and warm, urging her head down toward her knees. She was perched on the edge of the passenger's seat, and he was crouched on the curb in front of her.

"I'm okay," she protested weakly, although she wasn't at all sure that was true. Her head still felt fuzzy, and there was the oddest flip-flopping sensation in her stomach that seemed to increase with the gentle pressure of Jason's fingers against her nape.

"Just relax," he insisted, his voice soothing her frayed nerves. All these years, and he'd never quite lost the distinctive accent of the inner city where he'd grown up. But Caroline liked the inflection. It was a reminder of where he'd come from and just how tough he was. She really believed that with Jason around, nobody was going to get near enough to hurt her.

She drew in a shaky breath and raised her head enough to look at him. He was so close that for a moment, she was disconcerted. His skin was burnished to a warm hue from the sun, but up close, she could still see faint traces of the scars he'd borne as a teenager, which had made him seem so dangerous and mysterious to her. There was one that bisected his left eyebrow and another along the chiseled rise of his cheekbone, as if he'd taken a blow that had split the skin.

But it was his eyes that made it difficult for her to catch her breath. They were clear and pure, caught somewhere between green and gray. In the late afternoon sunlight, they appeared bottomless, and Caroline had a sense that if she looked deeply enough, she might even see the secrets that he tried so hard to keep.

"Hey," he said, peering up at her. "Sure you're okay?"

She nodded and tried to pull herself together. "Yes, thanks. I've never actually keeled over before. Sorry about that."

He lifted one shoulder in a half shrug. "It's not an uncommon reaction, although it could have easily been avoided." He arched one eyebrow in a look that clearly said he'd warned her. "Once the investigators are finished, I'll send out a team to clean up."

"Hey, boss, everything okay?"

Still on his haunches, Jason turned to look at his deputy. "Yeah, we're good. I'm going to take Ms. Banks to the hotel and get her something to eat." He shifted his attention back to Caroline. "Are you feeling up to a drive?"

She didn't think she'd ever eat again. The image of the bloodstained threshold haunted her. She stared at Jason with a growing sense of respect.

"How do you do this?"

He didn't pretend to misunderstand, and his eyes softened fractionally. "By doing whatever it takes."

Before Caroline could respond, Deputy Black stepped toward the car, his entire body on full alert. Immediately, Jason rose to his feet, pushing her into the car and closing the door, before planting himself directly outside her window.

One of the police officers quickly crossed the lawn toward them. "That's Marisola Perez, the neighbor's housekeeper. We've already cleared her."

Caroline peered through the window to see a woman walking down the driveway that bordered her father's property. She looked to be in her forties, and she wore a simple cotton dress with an apron that reminded her of the uniforms worn by hotel maids.

The woman clutched her purse and walked with her head down, clearly uncomfortable with the activity going on next door and the attention that was suddenly focused on her. When she reached the end of the driveway and turned onto the sidewalk, she cast one quick glance toward Jason and the car.

"Have a good evening, ma'am," Deputy Black said.

She gave a jerky nod, and Caroline watched as Ms. Perez quickly crossed the road and climbed into an older model sedan, then drove away. Only when the car was out of sight did Jason and Deputy Black relax.

"Freaking rich people," the police officer said in a disparaging tone. "Every house on the street has a gardener, a housekeeper, a cook and a personal assistant. I guess when you have money, you lose the ability to do anything for yourself." He shook his head in disgust. "Christ, there's more hired help on this street than there are actual residents. Just questioning them is going to take us days."

There was an uncomfortable silence, and the officer suddenly became aware of Caroline sitting in the car, staring at him in astonishment through the open window.

"Beg your pardon, ma'am," he mumbled, and twin splotches of color appeared high on his cheeks.

With an embarrassed glance at Jason, he turned and hurried back to the house. Jason and Deputy Black exchanged quiet words that Caroline couldn't hear; then the deputy strode toward his own vehicle.

Troubled by the man's words, she looked around her at the houses on the street. Many of the nearby residents had come to stand on their front porches or lawns, drawn by the excessive number of police officers and news reporters. She knew from experience that this was a quiet neighborhood. Nothing exciting ever happened in Sea Cliff, unless it was a black-tie dinner party and the governor was invited. To have a prominent and respected member of the community gunned down on his own front steps was beyond shocking.

As Caroline noted the residents who stood watching, she realized that what the police officer had said was true.

She could easily spot the housekeepers and nannies who had come out to the street to watch, conspicuous because of their uniforms.

She'd never considered it odd to have hired help while she was growing up. As a child, they'd had a live-in cook and a woman who came to the house twice a week to clean. There was a man who took care of the landscaping and another who took care of their swimming pool. Her father had an assistant who spent most of his time at the house. Even when William had been at work, Caroline had never been alone.

But what must that kind of lifestyle look like to a guy whose career was in public service? Caroline didn't blame the officer for what he'd said. From his perspective, it probably did appear that the residents of Sea Cliff were incapable of caring for themselves.

After a moment, Jason came around to the driver's side. He'd taken off his sports coat at the hospital, and he made no effort to hide his gun, which he wore in a shoulder holster. She wondered if he was sending a deliberate message to anyone who might be watching the house, or her. She admitted to finding this new Jason a little intimidating. He'd always been the strong, silent type, but combined with a don't-mess-with-me attitude and a firearm, he was positively forbidding.

He started the car and then turned in his seat to look at her. "I'm sorry about what that officer said. You shouldn't have to listen to that. Everyone has the right to earn a living, and the people in this neighborhood provide good jobs and income for a lot of families. Sure you're okay?"

"Yes, I'm fine. And he has a right to his opinion. That woman—" She stopped, feeling foolish.

Jason waited, expectant. "Yes?"

"Your men interviewed her?"

"Both the police and the FBI did, yes."

"I see. I was wondering…have they already interviewed my father's housekeeper? And gardener? I mean, they'd have opportunity. They know his schedule, right? They know when he's home alone."

"The police and the FBI have spoken with his housekeeper. Her name is Consuela Garcia, and she's about seventy years old. She's worked for your father for almost five years, and she has a rock-solid alibi for last night. He also has a gardener, who happens to be Consuela's husband." He paused. "They're good people, Caroline. You don't have to worry. They'd do anything for your father, and they're devastated by what happened to him."

"Thank you. I'm sorry to sound so suspicious." She flashed him an embarrassed smile. "I know this is what you do and that your men have everything under control. I guess I'm just feeling a little paranoid."

"That's good. That means you're on alert and you'll be more aware of your surroundings. Once we get to the hotel, we'll go through some safety guidelines."

The hotel was only blocks from the hospital, and Caroline wasn't surprised to discover that Jason had sent one of his men ahead to register and retrieve the room key. The Fairmont was one of the most exclusive hotels in San Francisco, and their room was located in one of the luxurious towers. If they hadn't just come from the scene of her father's shooting, she might have thought Jason was being a little dramatic in how he carefully surveyed their surroundings as they made their way to the room. She found herself reassured, both by his vigilance and his strong, steady presence.

Colton Black opened the door at Jason's curt knock, and Caroline found herself ushered into the room. She looked around, more than a little surprised at the size of the suite. She'd expected a studio, with a small living area and kitchenette and an adjoining bedroom. The suite of rooms that Jason had reserved was enormous, with a spacious parlor area and two private bedrooms. There was a fireplace, flanked by deep bookshelves, and a wet bar. A telescope stood in front of the wraparound windows, and the furnishings were rich and lush. Caroline turned to stare wordlessly at Jason.

He shrugged and walked across the room to the closest bedroom. He set her small suitcase down just inside the door. "We need a space large enough to accommodate the two of us, without you feeling like I'm right on top of you."

His tone was casual, but his words conjured up decadent images of the two of them, naked and tangled in her bedsheets. A peek inside the bedroom only ramped up her lustful imaginings. An enormous bed dominated the room, heaped high with pillows. Through a wide door, she could see a spectacular marble bathroom equipped with a whirlpool tub and a flat-screen television. Pushing aside her own inappropriate thoughts, she turned back to Jason.

"Who's paying for this?" she asked. "And don't try to

tell me that the U.S. Marshals Service provides five-star hotels for their clients."

Jason scowled. "Don't worry about it, okay?"

"Is this coming out of your own pocket?" When he tried to move away, Caroline stepped in front of him. "Is it?"

He looked resigned as he unfastened his shoulder holster with practiced fingers and removed it, then set the harness and weapon down on a nearby table. "The only thing you should be concerned about is your father. Nothing else."

"Jason—"

"I can afford it." His voice clearly said the conversation was over.

"Seriously, he can." This came from Colton Black, who stood near the door, watching the exchange with amusement. "Hey, boss, I'm going to set up outside."

Jason nodded. "Let me know when you change shifts with Deputy Mitchell."

"Will do."

Colton stepped out of the room, closing the door firmly behind him and leaving Caroline alone with Jason. She watched as he locked the door, deliberately avoiding any eye contact with her.

"Where is Deputy Black going to sleep?"

"He and Deputy Mitchell have a room across the hall. They'll take turns watching the corridor and the stairwell."

"And you'll stay here? With me?"

He turned to look at her. "You bet."

"For how long?"

"However long it takes."

"You're sacrificing a lot, coming up to San Francisco to babysit me." She picked up a small decorative bowl from an end table and turned it over in her hands, pretending to study it. "Doesn't your girlfriend object?"

A ghost of a smile touched his lips, and Caroline knew her pathetic attempt to find out about his personal life had been completely transparent.

When he didn't answer, Caroline put the bowl back and sank down onto the nearest sofa with a weary sigh. She didn't know how she was going to bear Jason Cooper's company for the next few days, or for however long it might take for authorities to catch the shooter. She only knew that the years had done nothing to diminish her attraction to him. If anything, she found him even more sexy and appealing than she had as a teenager.

Part of her was appalled by her reaction to him. She should be thinking about her father and what she could do to help him, not what she could do to get Jason into her bed. Especially when he'd made it abundantly clear that he didn't hold her in very high esteem. She knew how close he was with her father, and although he hadn't said anything, she suspected he was all too aware of how seldom she'd returned to the bay area to visit. How would he react if he knew that one of the reasons she hadn't returned to San Francisco was because she didn't want to risk an encounter with him? She needed to maintain her distance from him, but she doubted her ability to hide her feelings from Jason, especially if they were going to be living together. But there was no way she'd ever give him the opportunity to reject her again.

Realistically, she knew she should be grateful to Jason for volunteering to protect her. He had an important job as a U.S. marshal in San Diego, and it couldn't have been easy for him to leave his district and travel to San Francisco to watch over her.

"I'm sorry," she finally said, raising her head. Jason had come to stand at the end of the sofa. The windows were behind him, and, although it was growing dark outside, they hadn't turned on any interior lights and she couldn't read his expression. "I'm sure this is hard for you, too."

"You have no idea."

His wry tone caused Caroline to look sharply at him, unable to tell if he was joking or not. Before she could ask him what he meant, he turned away.

"I asked Deputy Black to order room service for us. Nothing fancy—a couple of steak sandwiches and salads."

Caroline wasn't hungry, but knew she should eat something. "Thanks. A salad is fine."

Jason arched an eyebrow and swept his gaze over her in one all-encompassing look that missed nothing. His cell phone rang, and he gave a grunt before turning away to speak quietly into the phone. Caroline sighed and pushed herself to her feet, then wandered to the tall bank of windows. Below she could see the city streets and beyond that the shimmering water of San Francisco Bay beneath the setting sun.

A few moments later, Jason came to stand beside her. "I said earlier that there were some safety rules we should go over, and one of the most important is to stay away from windows. You make yourself an easy target for any-one outside, especially at night."

"You think there's someone standing down there, watching the hotel?" she asked in disbelief.

"No," he admitted. "Not here, but while we're at the hospital, I think it's better you not go near the windows. Until we know what we're dealing with, I'm not taking any chances. Second rule, don't answer the phone or the door. I'll do that. Third, you don't go anywhere without me. If we're at the hospital, you don't even go to the rest-room unless I'm with you. Got it?"

Caroline hugged herself around the middle, feeling a chill wash over her. "You're scaring me, Jason."

To her surprise, he took her by the shoulders and turned her toward him, dipping his head to look directly into her eyes. "I'm not going to let anything happen to you, okay? As long as I'm with you, you're safe."

Before she could respond, he pulled her against him, enfolding her in his arms. He felt so solid and strong that Caroline instinctively hugged him back. His woodsy scent transported her back to being sixteen years old. Desire hit her like a sledgehammer, and she drew in a ragged breath, intensifying her hold on him. Beneath the crisp fabric of his shirt, she felt his muscles bunch and tighten.

"Caroline…" His voice was a husky rasp against her ear.

Lifting her face, she met his gaze. For just an instant, she saw the raw hunger in his eyes, and his expression gave her courage. She couldn't deny that she'd thought about kissing Jason far more than she should have since he'd first walked through the door of her law firm. Fixing her attention on his mouth, she told herself she would give him one kiss, just to thank him for everything he'd done. There was no harm in a simple gesture of gratitude, was there?

Slowly, she reached up and pressed a light kiss against the corner of his mouth. He made a strangled sound in his throat but didn't release her. Emboldened, she brushed her lips gently against his. For a brief instant, there was no response, and then he gave a groan of defeat and his arms tightened around her. His hand slid up between her shoulder blades to pull her closer, and he slanted his mouth hard over hers.

The kiss was so deep and so carnal that Caroline's legs went a little weak. She melted into him, welcoming the hot, slick slide of his tongue against hers. He reached up, released her hair clip and dropped it onto the floor, then fisted his hand in her hair and tugged her head to one side. Pulling his mouth away, he trailed his lips along the line of her jaw, to the tender spot just beneath her ear. Caroline took in big gulps of air and shivered with pleasure. When he skated his mouth along the length of her neck, she gave a faint moan and clutched him closer, her fingers digging into the firm muscles of his back.

As he bent her slightly back over his arm and feasted on the sensitive skin of her throat, Caroline forgot almost everything except the way he made her feel. In that moment, she realized that her life wasn't the only thing at risk.

4

JASON DIDN'T KNOW if he'd have had the ability to do the right thing and push Caroline away.

Again.

Thankfully, a knock sounded on the door, dragging him back to his senses, and he reluctantly released her. Looking a little dazed, she moistened her lips and pressed her hands against her flushed cheeks. Drawing in a deep breath, he retrieved his weapon from the table and strode to the door. Peering through the peephole, he saw Colton standing in the corridor with a rolling tray of food. With a quick glance at Caroline, who had turned away, he shoved the gun into the back of his waistband and opened the door.

"I've checked everything," Colton said, indicating the tray. "Looks good."

"Order something for yourself and Deputy Mitchell," Jason told him.

"Will do, boss. Oh, one more thing. I spoke with Judge Banks's assistant, Steven Anderson, and he's bringing over copies of the case files that the judge was working on. Everything for the past year."

Jason nodded. "Okay, thanks. Does the FBI have any leads?"

"They found a partial footprint in the flower bed beside the front porch and sent it over to the lab for processing." The other man paused, his eyes sharpening on Jason. "Everything okay?"

He wondered how the other man would react if he told him that he'd just had Judge Banks's daughter—the woman he was sworn to protect—in a steamy liplock. Or that he'd likely be in bed with her right now if Colton hadn't chosen that moment to knock on the door. On the other hand, the deputy would probably find the whole thing highly entertaining. After all, he'd met his fiancée, Maddie, after she'd taken him hostage, stolen his truck and his service revolver and then led him on a chase through the Sierra Nevada mountains to Reno. Even after he'd caught her, Colton hadn't been able to actually arrest her. Instead, he'd fallen in love with her and asked her to marry him. Of course, there had been extenuating circumstances, and even Jason had found himself drawn into helping them.

But he couldn't see a happy ending for himself and Caroline, not when they came from such different backgrounds. Not when he owed her father so much. Not when he'd bruised her young heart twelve years ago.

He should never have asked for this protective detail. But the thought of letting anyone else take responsibility for her safety had been unthinkable. Quite simply, he didn't trust anyone to watch over her the way that he would.

"Is something amusing, sir?"

Colton's words snapped Jason out of his reverie, and he shook his head. "No, nothing about this situation is amusing. I'm just seeing the irony, that's all."

"What do you mean?"

That having him watch over Caroline Banks was a little like having the wolf guard the lamb. But he couldn't say that to his deputy marshal.

"Order yourself some supper, Deputy, and I'll see you around midnight."

"Yes, sir."

Jason drew the food into the room and closed the door, securing the chain and the dead bolt despite the fact that both Deputy Black and Deputy Mitchell sat directly outside. He was acutely conscious of Caroline watching him from the far side of the room. He exhaled roughly, and pinched the bridge of his nose.

"About what happened," he began, not looking at her. "That was a mistake."

"Which part?" she asked. "Kissing me or stopping?"

He slanted her a warning look. "Caroline."

"What if I didn't want you to stop?"

Her words reverberated through Jason, causing his body to harden. She'd felt so good in his arms, and she'd tasted exactly as he'd remembered from all those years ago, like wild honey. But she was no longer an impressionable, innocent girl. She was a woman now, and there was no reason why he shouldn't take whatever she offered. He'd be lying if he said he didn't want her.

He did.

He also knew that getting involved with Caroline would be a mistake of monumental proportions. After all, she was the precious daughter of his mentor and friend. Judge Banks had spent his life ensuring her safety and happiness. He wanted the best for her, and that didn't include a guy like Jason. He could still hear her scathing words from that long-ago night—he was gutter trash.

He may have cleaned up his act and donned the veneer of respectability, but deep down he knew she was right. He couldn't change who he was—the son of a drug addict, born and raised on the crime-ridden streets of Hunters Point. He'd done things that would cause Caroline to recoil in disgust if she ever knew.

Even if he could change who he was, it would make no difference. They lived on opposite sides of the country, and he didn't do long-distance relationships any more than he did long-term relationships.

"Look," he finally said, carefully choosing his words, "you've had a traumatic day, and you're vulnerable right now. I won't take advantage of you that way, not when I'm detailed to protect you."

"Even if it's what I want?"

Jason felt a wry smile tug at his mouth. Even now, after all these years, she felt entitled to have something simply on the basis of wanting it.

"I'm not sure you know what you want right now."

Her mouth tightened, and he could almost see the walls going up around her. She was shutting down, shutting him out. "I want to go home."

He gave her a tolerant look. "Caroline, you know that's

not possible. Not right now. Maybe in a day or two, if they clear the scene."

Her chin went up. "What about the beach house? That's not off-limits, is it?"

He frowned. "The beach house is no safer than the house in Sea Cliff. We have to assume that whoever shot your father also knows about the house in Santa Cruz. Even if we cleared the house, it's a long drive. Sure you want to make that trip each day?"

"So I could stay there?" she asked, ignoring his question.

Jason didn't like the idea of returning to the beach house, but there was no reason why she couldn't return home, either to the house in Sea Cliff, once the investigators were finished processing the crime scene, or the house in Santa Cruz. He had enough men to provide ample security wherever she chose to go.

She stared at him for a moment, then spun on her heel and walked toward the windows. She abruptly changed course and moved to stand near the table.

"Please tell me we can go to the beach house. Even you can see that I can't stay here," she said, not looking at him.

With you.

She didn't say the words aloud, but they hung in the air between them. Jason blew out a hard breath. This was his fault, and he mentally kicked himself. But there was no way he was going to give up the protection detail or allow another deputy to step in and take over. He'd pulled a lot of strings when he'd contacted his counterpart in San Francisco and asked for the assignment. He couldn't back out now. And in all honesty, he didn't want to. "The investigators should be done with the Sea Cliff house in a day or so," he said quietly. "If you want to go to the house in Santa Cruz, I'll make the arrangements. But for tonight, we'll stay here."

Her cell phone rang, and she reached for it, glancing at the screen before looking at him. "I have to take this call. I'll stay here for tonight if there's no other choice. But I'm checking out tomorrow morning."

"Caroline—"

She'd already turned away, putting the phone to her ear as she strode into the bedroom. Before she shut the door, he heard her say, "Hi, Patrick. I'm sorry—I meant to call you earlier."

Who was Patrick? A coworker? A friend? Or something more? Jason scrubbed a hand over his face, blocking out the image of Caroline with another man. Over the years, he'd managed to work her into his conversations with the judge, so he always knew what was going on in her life. But William had never talked about Caroline's boyfriends. Jason hadn't pressed him, because he wasn't sure he really wanted to know. Pulling out his own phone, he made a call to the officer on duty at the hospital, reassuring himself that the judge was still alive and that he'd had no visitors since they had left. Then he made a call to Agent Sullivan, the lead investigator on the FBI team, to get more information about the footprint they had recovered.

He was still on the phone when Caroline came out of the bedroom thirty minutes later and quietly sat down to eat her salad. Jason ended his conversation and studied her closely. Her face was blotchy, and her eyes were red-rimmed and puffy. He wondered if she'd had a heart-to-heart with Patrick, sharing her emotions with the other man the way she refused to with him. Jason pushed down a flare of jealousy, reminding himself that there was absolutely no reason why Caroline should share her feelings with him. He hadn't done anything to earn her trust. In fact, some might argue that he'd violated her trust in kissing her.

He sat down across from her and unwrapped the sandwich he'd ordered. They ate in silence for a moment, and Jason knew that Caroline was only going through the motions and wasn't actually enjoying her meal, or even tasting it. Truthfully, he wasn't all that interested in eating, either.

"Are you okay?" he finally asked.

CAROLINE RAISED HER head to look at him and nodded. "Yes. It's just been a long day."

That was the truth. She felt drained, physically and emotionally. After the flight from Virginia, and the three-hour difference in time, she was exhausted. Then Patrick Dougherty had called. He'd seen the reports of the shooting on the evening news. Although he'd purportedly called to offer his sympathy and find out how she was doing, Caroline suspected what he really wanted to find out was how long she planned to be away. Devon Lawton needed legal representation, and she was one of the few pro bono lawyers who knew the kid's full history. Caroline felt guilty leaving Devon in the lurch, but right now she had no other option. She'd asked Patrick to call the district attorney's office and have them assign legal representation for Devon. Tomorrow morning she'd call one of the paralegals at her law firm and have them bring her case files over to the new lawyer. Right now, that was the best she could do.

"I called the hospital," Jason said, interrupting her thoughts. "There's been no change in your father's condition." He nodded toward her salad. "The best thing you can do is eat and then get some sleep. We'll head over early to see him."

Caroline knew he was right. While she wanted to be at the hospital with her father, realistically she knew there was nothing she could do. He was in good hands, and she had to hope that his condition would improve over the next few days. But she couldn't dispel the feelings of helplessness and guilt that had plagued her since she'd learned her father had been shot in cold blood on his front doorstep. She wanted to do something useful, something that would help him. She didn't want to sit in a hotel room, a virtual prisoner. And she definitely did not want Jason Cooper as her bodyguard.

"Did the police find anything at the house that might give them a lead?"

"Just the partial footprint in the flower bed. But there's no guarantee that it belongs to the person who did this. Your father employs a lawn care service, so it could have been left by a worker."

Caroline pushed her plate away. "So exactly what's your role in all of this? Are you only here to watch over me, or will you also help in the investigation? I mean, it would be pretty hard to just sit by and not have an active role, right?"

"I do have an active role," he said quietly. "My role is protecting you."

"But you're a U.S. marshal. Don't you usually give this kind of job to your deputies?" She leaned forward. "Why don't you assign one of your men—Deputy Black, maybe—to stay with me? Then you can do whatever it is you do to find the sonofabitch who did this to my father."

She watched as he pushed his own plate aside and gave her a crooked smile. That slight tilting of his mouth fascinated her, and Caroline realized how seldom she'd seen Jason smile. She didn't even know what his laughter sounded like. During her youth, when he had come over to the house to see her father, she couldn't recall a single time when he'd been lighthearted or full of exuberance. She'd never given it much thought, because part of his appeal had been his dark intensity and the aura of danger that had clung to him.

He was still broody and intense, but she hadn't sensed any of the pent-up rage he'd once exhibited, except when he'd first seen her father at the hospital. But she understood that anger, because she felt it, too. Now she wondered if he'd managed to find happiness in the past twelve years. He'd certainly achieved an impressive level of success in his career.

"Do you like your job?" she asked, intercepting whatever he might have said in response to her suggestion that he switch assignments with Deputy Black. "I mean, is it everything you'd hoped it would be?"

He gave her a bemused look, and then his smile broadened. "Yeah, it is. In fact, it's even better than I'd imagined."

"Tell me about it."

To Caroline's astonishment, he actually seemed a little embarrassed. "Nah. You don't want to hear about my job. I'll have you bored to tears within minutes."

She doubted that very much. The one thing Jason had never made her feel was bored.

Aroused? Frustrated and angry? Yes. But never bored.

His smiled faded, and she saw his expression change to concern. "Hey. Are you sure you're okay?"

"I'm fine. It was just a shock to see so much blood...." Her voice trailed off, and she looked down at her hands, blinking back sudden tears. "I should have been here. I should never have moved so far away."

Reaching across the table, Jason caught her chin in his fingers and tipped her face up so that she was forced to look at him. "You have every right to live your own life, and your father didn't want it any other way. He's always been proud of you and what you've accomplished. You're working for one of the best law firms in Virginia."

Caroline pulled away. "It's mostly just divorce and child custody cases," she demurred. "Nothing exciting."

She couldn't say why, but she was reluctant to tell him about her work with Virginia's Child Protective Services, or how most of her time was dedicated toward safeguarding the rights of abused and neglected children. She was afraid if she did tell him, he'd realize the impact he'd had on her life, and she didn't want to give him that kind of power. He'd once called her spoiled and selfish, and she preferred to let him believe that. It would be easier to keep him at a distance.

"Do you enjoy it?"

"Sometimes it's emotionally grueling," she admitted, thinking of Devon's case, "but I can't imagine doing anything else."

"Family law, huh?" he mused, his lips twitching. "Who would have thought?"

Caroline flushed. "There's actually quite a bit of casework involved. And we're talking wealthy clients. You can't take that lightly."

"Of course not. Do they pay you well?"

"I get by." Caroline thought of her small apartment in a modest section of the city. If she accepted the job offer from the district attorney's office, she'd need to find more affordable housing, or advertise for a roommate. The cut in pay that came with that job meant she wouldn't be able to stay in her apartment without making some lifestyle changes. But the thought of downsizing didn't alarm her. She'd done a lot of growing up since she'd left for Richmond, and she'd realized that material wealth no longer gave her the same pleasure it had when she was young.

Jason frowned, reading her expression. "If you're struggling, why wouldn't you just ask the judge to help you? Christ, Caroline, you have a trust fund."

"I don't want to rely on my father or on my trust fund," she replied. "I want to succeed on my own merits, the same way you did."

He leaned forward, and she saw a muscle flex in his jaw. "You think I got here on my own?" he asked. "If it weren't for your father, I'd be dead or in prison. I only got this far because of him. He literally saved my life."

She made a dismissive noise. "That's not what I mean. He might have pointed you in the right direction, but you did the rest on your own."

Jason lounged back in his chair and considered her. "So you're telling me that you don't dip into your trust fund at all?"

Hearing the disbelief in his voice, Caroline raised her chin. "It's true. I haven't touched a cent of it since I was in college."

"So you're spending your salary on—what?" He indicated her outfit. "Clothes? Because even a simple guy like me knows designer clothing when I see it."

"I buy this stuff secondhand. You'd be surprised how many upscale consignment shops there are in Richmond, and how many prominent women use them." She narrowed her eyes at him. "You think because my father is wealthy that I just blow through money? That I spend all my free time shopping?"

He held up his hands in surrender. "Okay, I'm sorry. I just seem to remember that you spent a lot of time at the mall as a teenager, and you'd come home with more shopping bags than you could carry. I just assumed that you use your trust fund to underwrite your current lifestyle. If that's not the case, then I apologize. No offense intended."

She narrowed her eyes at him. "You once accused me of being spoiled and getting whatever I wanted—"

He shot her a quelling look, causing her to clamp her mouth shut.

"You did," she insisted, after a long moment, keeping her tone cool. "That last night at the beach house, when I was sixteen. You said my problem was that I always got whatever I wanted, even when it wasn't good for me."

He stared at her, his expression dark. "Caroline, whatever I said that night, I said out of self-preservation. You were sixteen. I would have said anything to get you to leave me alone."

She gave a bitter laugh. "Whatever. I wasn't woman enough for you, right? My boobs weren't big enough, and I had no experience. Why bother with a scrawny teenage virgin when you could have a real woman, right?"

Jason made a growling sound of annoyance and rose to his feet. Planting his hands on the table, he leaned toward her, and it took all Caroline's resolve not to cringe from the heat and anger she saw reflected in his eyes. She stared boldly back at him instead.

"Is that what you think?" he said through gritted teeth. "Well, here's the truth. I was barely holding it together that night. If you hadn't left when you did, I would have had you on your back in that bed, and I would have screwed you blind. I would have taken you six ways to Sunday, and I wouldn't have given a rat's ass about your virginity, or the fact that I owed your father everything. I would have hurt you, Caroline, and in the morning, I would have been gone."

For a moment, she was too stunned to speak. His crude depiction had her imagination surging with lurid images of what might have happened that night. The vehemence in his voice almost made her believe him.

"Well," she said when she could finally speak. "At least that's better than thinking you didn't want me."

"But I didn't," he continued, his voice harsh. "Oh, I wanted your hot little body, but I didn't want you. I didn't want a girlfriend or a relationship, and if you think that's where we were headed, you are deluding yourself."

Even after all these years, his words had the ability to inflict pain. Here, finally, was a glimpse of the angry, dangerous youth he had once been. "So where *were* we headed?"

He laughed sardonically. "To hell, sweetheart. Because I would have used you and then left. You would have tried to put a good face on it, but every time my name came up in conversation, it would have felt like someone twisting a knife in your gut. And if by some miracle I hadn't gotten you pregnant, you still wouldn't have been able to hide the truth from your father." A muscle twitched in his jaw. "He would have learned what happened, and if he didn't have me arrested for statutory rape, he would have found another way to ruin me. And in time, I'd have grown to hate you almost as much as you hated me."

The picture he painted was so cruel and so bleak that Caroline felt tears prick the back of her eyelids. Her voice, when she spoke, was little more than a whisper. "You really would have hated me?"

"Without a doubt," he assured her. "But not nearly as much as I would have hated myself."

5

JASON HADN'T BEEN back to the beach house in Santa Cruz since the night he'd found Caroline waiting for him in his bed. The place hadn't changed much in twelve years, and despite the fact that he and Caroline had hardly spoken through the course of the long day, some of the tightness in his chest eased as he walked through the spacious house and onto the back deck, which overlooked the beach and the crashing surf.

The sun was beginning to set over the water, streaking the sky with brilliant reds and pinks. Several couples walked along the water's edge, letting the waves lap at their feet. To the right of the deck, standing near the dunes, he could just make out Colton's shadowy figure.

Deputy Black, Deputy Mitchell and three other officers had arrived earlier to get the layout of the house and evaluate the security. Even now, they stood guard both inside and on the surrounding property. Jason hoped that he and Caroline wouldn't be here for more than a couple of days. He liked the house, but he didn't relish the long drive back and forth to the hospital, with Caroline silent and cold beside him.

He knew he'd hurt her feelings with the ugly picture he'd painted for her, but he needed her to understand that when he'd turned her away twelve years ago, he'd done it for her own sake. And for his.

Truth was, he'd lied when he'd told her that he would have hurt her. That he would have left her. That he would have hated her.

But the reality was that she'd been much too young. There had been no chance that they could have had any kind of relationship, even if her father would have allowed it, which he wouldn't have. Not then. Maybe not even now.

Jason thought of the cases he'd recently worked in San Diego, involving some of the worst kinds of criminals. While he felt a certain satisfaction in putting them behind bars, he also experienced a sense of guilt, because on some level, he related to those lowlifes. Under different circumstances, it could have been him behind bars. He knew that some of the people he worked with were aware of his background and looked down their noses at him because of it. As much as he tried to tell himself that his past experiences made him a better law enforcement officer, he couldn't shake the sense that he'd never completely eradicated the angry delinquent kid that he'd once been. He was just better at hiding it.

Caroline had once accused him of keeping his tattoos concealed because of what others might think about him. In truth, he couldn't care less what anyone thought about him, but he took no pride in the ink he'd gotten as a teenager. There were times he'd even considered having the tattoos removed, but he had decided to keep them as a reminder of who he really was. He could fool some people, but he couldn't fool himself.

He leaned forward, bracing his forearms on the railing of the deck, and breathed in the clean, salt-tinged air. Now that Caroline was living in Virginia, the judge rarely spent any time at the beach house. He refused to sell it, however, despite the fact he could get a small fortune for the oceanfront property. The house had belonged to his late wife, who had died in a car crash when Caroline was just a toddler. William had always maintained that the house was part of Caroline's inheritance.

Being back at the beach house only served to remind Jason that he and Caroline came from different worlds. He didn't like to think about his own parents, or his miserable childhood in Hunters Point, one of the most impoverished and crime-ridden districts of San Francisco.

He only knew that if it hadn't been for Judge Banks, he probably wouldn't have survived to adulthood. He hadn't been back to his old neighborhood since he'd turned eighteen. He hadn't seen his old man since he was twenty, when his father had turned up at his college dormitory looking to borrow money. He could still recall the anger and shame he'd felt when he'd opened his door to see Daryl Cooper outside his room, looking like a homeless bum and obviously in need of his next fix. Jason had wanted him gone before any of the other guys in the dorm saw him and guessed who he was and where Jason had come from.

But everything in him had rebelled against giving his

father money, especially when he knew it would only go toward drugs or alcohol. Only when Daryl had grown belligerent and threatened to make a scene had Jason relented. He'd given his father everything he'd had, under the condition that he never come back and never try to get in touch with him again.

That had been almost fifteen years ago, and he hadn't seen Daryl Cooper since. But the memory of that exchange remained vivid. Even now, there were times when he felt his life was a sham and that sooner or later people would realize he was nothing more than poor white trash.

He turned at the sound of footsteps behind him and saw Deputy Mitchell and another man just inside the house. He recognized the second man as Steven Anderson, the judge's legal assistant. They'd met several times when Jason had traveled to San Francisco to visit the judge. He was young, probably in his mid-twenties, and he reminded Jason of the ambitious Stanford law students who had frequented Judge Banks's house back when he was a teenager: good-looking, affluent and entitled. As Steven pushed a two-wheeled dolly, stacked high with white cardboard boxes, Jason couldn't help thinking that the legal assistant looked as if he'd be more comfortable on a golf course than in a courtroom.

He stepped through the French doors into the house and shook Steven's hand.

"Thanks for bringing these over on such short notice," he said. "I'll make sure you get them back as soon as possible."

Steven nodded. "No problem. I had our paralegals working around the clock to make copies of everything before the FBI confiscated the files. This is every case the judge worked on for the past twelve months." He indicated one box with an orange label on the outside. "These are the high-profile cases, like the Sanchez case and the Conrad Kelly case."

Conrad Kelly was the leader of an antigovernment extremist group, and he'd been found guilty of bombing numerous state and federal buildings in California over a ten-year time span. He'd been convicted earlier that year, and Judge Banks had sentenced him to thirty years in prison. As a result, the judge had received several death threats, but subsequent investigations had led nowhere.

"Got it," he said to the other man, lifting the top box and placing it on the nearby dining table. "I'll start with this box."

Steven hesitated.

Jason paused in the process of opening the box. "Was there something else?"

The legal assistant shifted his weight. "No. It's just that the judge dealt with a lot of slimeballs. It could have been any one of them. But—"

"But what?"

Steven looked embarrassed. "It's probably nothing, but there was this one night a few weeks ago, when I was at the judge's house. We were reviewing a case that's coming to trial in another week." Seeing Jason's expression, he hurried on. "Anyway, as I was leaving that night, there was this car parked outside the house, with someone inside. I didn't think too much of it, other than the car definitely didn't belong in a neighborhood like Sea Cliff. But it took off when I came down the walkway toward the sidewalk. I didn't get a look at the driver."

Jason frowned. "When was this, exactly?"

"Almost three weeks ago, on Wednesday night at ten."

"Do you remember the make or model of the car? Could you determine the color?"

"No. I'm not much of a car aficionado, so the best I can tell you is that it was a shit-box sedan, either brown or greenish-brown. But I noticed that one of the taillights wasn't working." He made an apologetic gesture. "I'm sorry—that's the best I can tell you. Like I said, it might not mean anything."

"Or it could mean everything." This from Colton, who had come in behind the other man. "Did you tell any of this to the police?"

Steven nodded. "Yeah, of course. I mentioned it when they came to the office to look at the judge's casework. They said they'd look into it."

"Thank you, Steven." Jason shook the other man's hand. "Deputy Black will show you out."

Steven hesitated. "Is, uh, Judge Banks's daughter here? I mean, that's why you're here, right? Speaking of which, why would she choose to stay in Santa Cruz and not in San Francisco? I'd think she'd want to be closer to her father." He gave a self-conscious laugh. "I haven't seen her since she graduated. Would be nice to say hello."

Jason exchanged a look with Colton. "Thanks again for coming by. I appreciate you making the drive, and I'll make sure you get the files back once we're done."

He was glad when the other man took the hint and left. Wasting no time, he opened the first box and began methodically removing the case files, laying them all out on the table. He looked up brusquely when Colton returned.

"I want everything you can find on Steven Anderson. How long he's worked for the judge, and what his relationship is to the family. And to Caroline."

Colton nodded. "Yes, sir. Probably nothing more than a youthful crush. She's the boss's daughter, after all, and she's very attractive. I'll bet all the judge's interns were panting after her back when she lived here. Anderson seems pretty benign."

Privately, Jason agreed. "Not taking any chances," he said evenly.

"Got it."

When Colton departed, Jason glanced toward the stairs. Caroline had claimed a headache and had gone straight to her room when they'd arrived at the beach house. He didn't doubt that she was exhausted; they had spent the entire day at the hospital with her father, and the ride to Santa Cruz had seemed endless, especially since she had refused to speak with him. Jason had never considered himself much of a conversationalist, and there were few things he hated more than meaningless chit-chat. So aside from a few questions related to whether the air-conditioning was sufficient or if she needed to stop and take a break, they hadn't spoken at all. But he'd been acutely aware of her during the long drive. He'd heard every soft sigh, noticed every shift of position in the seat next to him, and had to keep his hands firmly on the steering wheel to prevent himself from reaching over to cover her fingers with his own. In short, the drive had been sheer torture.

Outside, the sun had disappeared over the horizon, and he walked deliberately through the house, checking the windows and doors. Upstairs, he paused outside Caroline's room to listen, but there was no sound from inside. He moved down the hall to the guest room and opened the door. This was his room when he stayed at the beach house, and seeing it now brought the events of that long-ago summer night rushing back.

He could still see Caroline, so sweet and tempting, wearing nothing but a pair of lacy panties. If he closed his eyes, he could even feel her skin...taste her lips...smell the fragrance of coconut and honeysuckle. The room hadn't changed at all in the past twelve years, and for just a moment, he thought he could smell the exotic-scented skin lotion that Caroline wore. With a stifled groan, he closed the door and went back downstairs.

It was almost ten o'clock, but Jason knew he'd never get to sleep. He rarely went to bed before 1:00 a.m., a habit that Caroline would no doubt say he'd gotten from her father. He pulled the folders out of the first box and sorted quickly through them until he found the case files he was looking for. He spent the next several hours poring through the documents, trying to decipher any clues that might hint at who had shot Judge Banks.

He was so absorbed in his work that he didn't hear the soft pad of footsteps behind him until it was too late. He caught a faint whiff of coconut and whirled in his chair. Except for the small table lamp near his elbow, the house was steeped in darkness, but he could see Caroline clearly. She stood just outside the circle of lamplight, wearing a short white bathrobe that left her slender legs bare. Her blond hair fell loosely around her face and shoulders, and she hugged her arms around her middle.

"Caroline?" He pushed his chair back and rose to his feet. "What is it?"

She stared him, her eyes haunted in her pale face. "I couldn't sleep. I had a dream…"

Jason didn't move toward her. He didn't trust himself to touch her, not when she looked so vulnerable and everything in him wanted to haul her into his arms and assure her that he'd take care of her.

"Here," he said, indicating the nearby sofa. "Come sit down. I'll get you a drink."

"Where are Deputy Black and Deputy Mitchell?" she asked, looking around the silent house.

"Deputy Mitchell has the night shift. He'll keep watch in the patrol car tonight." He gestured toward the end of the hallway, where her father's bedroom and a second guest room were located. "Deputy Black is asleep in the guest room. He'll relieve Mitchell at dawn. You're safe, Caroline. Come sit down."

Obediently, she sat down on the sofa and curled her legs beneath her. He'd closed the doors that led to the deck but had opened the nearest window so that he could enjoy the cool ocean breezes. Realizing she was shivering, he pulled a cotton throw from the opposite end of the sofa and draped it around her shoulders before walking over to the wet bar.

He poured them each a glass of bourbon. After handing one to Caroline, he sat down beside her, carefully putting some space between them. She turned toward him on the cushions, and the blanket slipped enough to one side so that he caught a glimpse of one slim thigh. He took a hefty swig of his drink.

Caroline cradled her own glass in her hands. "I had a dream about my father." Her voice was low and troubled. "In the dream, I'm standing on the sidewalk when he opens the door. I can see that the person standing on the porch has a gun. I try to scream a warning, but nothing comes out."

"Caroline—"

"So I run toward the house, but my feet are so heavy, as if they're encased in concrete. All I can do is watch while he's shot. And there's so much blood...it spills down the steps in a gush, until it surrounds my feet."

She sobbed and covered her mouth with a trembling hand. Jason took her glass and set it down on the coffee table with his own. She didn't resist when he pulled her across the distance that separated them and enfolded her in his arms.

"Shh," he murmured against her hair. "It was just a dream. Your father is alive, and we'll find whoever did this to him."

Her fingers clutched at his shirt, and she shuddered with recalled horror. "It seemed so real. And when I woke up, I felt so helpless. So alone." She raised her face to look at him. "But then I remembered that you were here. And I knew everything would be okay."

Her words caused something to shift in Jason's chest, and he had to fight to keep his arms from tightening around her.

"Caroline—"

She swallowed, tears still shimmering in her eyes.

"I'm sorry I've been so miserable to you today. I just kept thinking about what you said last night, about hating me."

"I never said I hated you," he corrected her. "I said I would have grown to hate you if we had slept together back then. There's a big difference."

She nodded and fixed her gaze on the center of his chest. "You're right. But I don't think you would have actually hated me, just like you wouldn't have left me."

She sounded so sure of herself that Jason felt one corner of his mouth twitch in amusement. "Oh yeah? And why do you think that?"

"Because you always do the right thing, no matter the cost to yourself."

He stared at her. He'd done the right thing when he'd turned her away, and she would never know how much it had cost him.

"Unlike me," she continued. "I was the one who left. I'm the only family he has, and I left him. What's worse is that I did it for my own selfish reasons."

Two days ago, Jason would have agreed with her. But seeing her misery, and the genuine regret in her eyes, he couldn't bring himself to criticize her. Instead, he tipped her chin up so that she was forced to look at him.

"None of this is your fault," he assured her. "Chances are that even if you'd stayed in the area, you'd have had your own place, and your father still would have been alone that night. Or worse, you could have been living with your dad, and it might have been you who answered the door." He stroked his thumb along the curve of her cheek. "The only blame is on the bastard who pulled the trigger. There was nothing you could have done to prevent this, Caroline, and your father wouldn't want you blaming yourself."

They gazed at each other, and Jason was aware of his own heartbeat, throbbing hard and heavy through his veins. She was looking at him as if he was her own personal hero, and he knew that if he didn't release her, he was going to end up doing something he'd later regret.

"Jason," she murmured and curled her fingers around his wrist. He still had her chin between his thumb and forefinger, and now she closed her eyes and pushed her cheek into his palm. "Even after all these years, I wonder…"

"What?" His voice sounded a little hoarse. "What do you wonder?"

She opened her eyes and looked up at him through her lashes, and the expression in those luminous blue depths sent a tidal wave of desire crashing over him.

"What it would be like to be with you…to hold you inside me," she whispered.

He was way out of his depth, with no lifeline in sight, but he suddenly didn't care. If this was what drowning was like, he'd die a happy man.

6

CAROLINE WANTED TO weep with relief when Jason gave a small groan of defeat and bent his head to cover her mouth with his own. Like the day before, the kiss was deep and carnal, and it sent a dark thrill of longing through her. He tasted like bourbon, and Caroline found herself leaning into him, inviting him to explore her more fully. He angled her face for better access, sliding his tongue past her teeth to lick the damp recesses of her mouth and feast on her lips.

Caroline moaned, and then he was scooping her onto his lap, so that her legs dangled over his thighs and his arms cradled her against his chest.

Pulling slightly away, Jason gazed down at her. "This is crazy."

Winding her arms around his neck, Caroline pushed her fingers through his hair and drew his head back down until their lips were only fractionally apart. "Completely," she agreed.

"You should probably go to bed," Jason breathed.

"Yes, most definitely."

She kissed him, a fusing of lips and tongues, and Jason groaned again, feeling his body tighten in response. She shifted on his lap, her supple bottom pressing into his arousal. Turning, Jason lay her down on the cushions of the sofa and eased himself down beside her without ever breaking the kiss. She murmured her approval and urged him closer.

She felt so good in his arms, and although there was a part of him that knew what he was doing was a bad idea, he couldn't bring himself to stop. She arched against him, and he felt her tug the hem of his shirt up. When she smoothed her palms over his back and explored his skin, he pulled back enough to search her eyes.

"Are you sure about this?" His voice was a husky rasp.

She wet her lips, and her fingertips pressed into his spine, as if she was afraid he might try to leave. She kept her voice light, but Jason could hear an underlying tremor, as if she couldn't quite conquer her own nerves.

"I've been trying to get you into bed for twelve years," she said. "So, yes, I'm sure."

Jason couldn't suppress his amused smile, because the truth was she'd avoided him like the plague for the past twelve years. Even when she'd graduated from college and he'd driven up from San Diego to attend her graduation party, she hadn't approached him. At that point, he hadn't seen her in a couple of years and he'd been blown away by her blond good looks and her air of confidence. She'd finally grown up, and he'd wanted nothing more than to ask her out, but she'd been surrounded by a group of young men, all vying for her attention. Her parting words from that long-ago night had come back to him.

By the time your conscience decides I'm old enough, I'll have had a dozen other guys.

He had no idea if she'd made good on her threat, but he'd backed off and had left the party without speaking to her.

"That's not quite how I remember it," he replied with a tender smile. "But as long as you're sure..."

Without giving her a chance to protest, he pushed to his feet, pulling her with him.

"Where are we going?" she asked, letting him lead her through the darkened house toward the staircase.

"I am not going to make love to you on a couch," he said, leading her up to the second floor. He flashed her a quick smile. "At least not the first time."

In the upstairs corridor, he glanced at her closed bedroom door and then moved past it to the room where he always stayed when he visited the beach house. The room where Caroline had asked him to be her first. He knew he was years too late, but there was a bittersweet satisfaction in being back here with her.

He stepped inside and drew her in behind him, kicking the door closed with his foot and locking it. Colton was asleep downstairs, and Deputy Mitchell was on duty in the car outside. Either of them could come looking for him. What he was doing was wrong on so many levels, but he suddenly didn't care. He was the selfish one, because all he could think about was how badly he wanted Caroline.

Pale moonlight slanted in through the windows, illuminating the room. He could see her clearly, but he was unprepared when she turned and pushed him up against the closed door. Her hands slid beneath his shirt, and then she was shoving the fabric up. Cool air wafted over his heated skin.

"Take this off," she demanded. "I want to feel all of you."

Jason hesitated.

"I've already seen your tattoos," she reminded him, correctly interpreting his reluctance. "And I think they're hot."

Jason complied, yanking the shirt over his head and dropping it onto the floor. Then her hands were there, stroking over his chest and shoulders, tracing her fingertips over the intricate tattoos even as she pressed her mouth against him. *Jesus.* He thought he'd be the one doing the seducing, but he'd been wrong.

He buried his hands in her hair, relishing the texture of the silken mass between his fingers as she gripped his rib cage and traced a path over his skin with her tongue.

"Caroline." Her name escaped his mouth on a groan. "Let me."

He let his head fall back against the door, aware that his heartbeat was coming faster. She was working her way down his torso, planting moist kisses along the center of his chest and stomach, until she reached the waistband of his jeans. She glanced up at him once, and then her fingers deftly worked the buckle and the button before slowly drawing his zipper down. Jason sucked in a breath when her fingers brushed against his stomach, and she hooked her fingers into his waistband. She tugged the stretchy material down just enough so that she could stroke one finger over the engorged head of his penis.

That light, feathery touch nearly undid him. He couldn't ever recall feeling this way before, as if it were his first time. He was incredibly aroused, and although he'd never admit it, a little anxious. He wanted this to be perfect for her.

"Oh, Jason," she murmured. "You're so...so beautiful."

"Enough," he muttered and reached down to stop her hand from exploring him further. He pulled her upward. In two strides, he reached the bed, drawing her with him. Her arms slipped around his waist, and she pressed herself against his bare chest.

"You smell so good, just like I remembered." Her voice was low and sexy. "Why did you stop me? I want to touch you everywhere."

"I want that, too." He slid his hands up the length of her arms. "In fact, if you don't touch me, I think I might die."

She laughed, a huff of breath that washed over him and caused goose bumps to rise on his sensitized flesh. She gave him a gentle shove, forcing him back onto the mattress. Then she was straddling him, her hands braced on either side of his head. Her robe gaped open, and Jason realized she was almost nude and her gorgeous breasts were right there, practically in his face.

Jason drew her down, covering her mouth in a heated kiss. She trembled and leaned against him, until he could feel the swell of her breasts pressed against his chest. Heat lanced through him, and he deepened the kiss, sweeping his tongue inside her mouth. She met him with a beguiling fierceness that took his breath away, first spearing her tongue against his and then sucking on it, drawing it deeper. Her mouth was hot and succulent.

As he angled her face for better access, she lowered her body and then, sweet Mary, he could feel her, rubbing back and forth over his throbbing erection. The sensation was so exquisite, so pleasurable, he wasn't sure he could stand it. While he wasn't exactly a monk, it had been a long time since he'd been with anyone. His self-control was tenuous, at best.

Without giving her time to protest, he turned her beneath him in one swift, smooth movement. She let out a small sound of surprise but then settled back against the pillows with a sigh of delight and wound her arms around his neck, feasting on his mouth.

Oh, yeah, this was perfect, except that now she was arching against him, rotating her hips against his in an invitation that was unmistakable.

Jason dragged his mouth free and bent his forehead to hers, sucking in deep breaths. "Easy, sweetheart," he gasped. "I don't want to go too fast, and if you keep that up, I'm not going to last."

She gave him a bemused smile. "Really? But you're a marshal. I thought you guys were all about control."

He raised his head and looked down into her flushed face. Her blue eyes glinted in the moonlight, shimmering with arousal. Her mouth was swollen from his kisses, reminding him of a ripe strawberry. He wanted to bite her.

"Where you're concerned," he said, his voice husky, "I have no control."

It was the truth. He was breaking every rule in the book by coming upstairs with her and not maintaining a professional distance. He'd sworn to protect her, and here he was taking complete advantage of her. He could tell himself that his prior friendship with her father—and, to a lesser extent, with Caroline herself—made it okay, but he knew he was lying to himself. He wanted her more than he could ever recall wanting another woman. He'd wanted her that night when she'd been sixteen years old and had done her best to entice him, but that had been nothing compared with what he felt right now.

Raising himself on one elbow, he pushed aside the fabric of her silky robe, until the upper swell of her breast was revealed. She made no protest, but he heard her sharp intake of breath. He traced his fingertips over the creamy flesh, noting how her nipple tightened beneath the satin fabric. Jason paused to devour the sight and then dipped his head to brush his lips over the hardened nub before drawing her nipple into his mouth and suckling it gently. He heard Caroline whimper, and he laved the distended tip with his tongue.

"Please…please." Her whisper was ragged, and she cupped his face, dragging it upward so she could fasten her mouth against his and draw his very soul from between his lips.

That broken plea, combined with her molten kiss, was enough to push the last of his restraint over the edge. He'd intended to go slowly, to let her set the pace, but he hadn't counted on the intensity of his need for her. Heat spiraled downward through his midsection as he felt his control stretch thin.

"You drive me crazy, you know," he muttered against her lips. "That night that you waited for me in this room… I didn't want to stop, but you were so young. Afterwards, I couldn't stop thinking about you, imagining how you would taste…."

He slanted his mouth across hers, deepening the kiss, wanting to consume her, to eat her alive. She arched against him, sliding her hands up over his shoulders to pull him closer.

He needed to be closer, too, with nothing separating them. He wanted to feel her skin against his, to absorb her heat. He pushed her robe down the length of her arms, wanting it gone completely. She helped him by pulling her arms free, and then she was completely naked but for the miniscule scrap of white silk at her crotch.

He almost stopped breathing.

Then he filled his hands with her breasts, admiring how full and firm they were and how her nipples ripened beneath his fingers.

"Oh, God," she panted, shifting restlessly against him. "You have to touch me or, I swear, I'm just going to die."

"But I am touching you," he rasped, smiling against her neck.

"No, I mean—you have to touch me…there."

Her plea was desperate, and lust jackknifed through Jason. With a low groan, he claimed her mouth while at the same time he glided his hand down over the silken skin of her abdomen until he encountered the edge of her panties.

Caroline made an incoherent sound and covered his hand with her own, pushing it downward. Requiring no further invitation, Jason cupped her through the thin layer of silk. She was sweltering, and the fabric was damp with her desire. He could feel the contours of her folds through the insubstantial barrier, but it wasn't enough.

Pulling away from her, he reared up on his knees and positioned himself between her legs. Caroline watched him through half-closed eyes as he drew her panties down over her hips. She helped him by drawing her legs up and kicking the filmy material free. And then, there she was, completely exposed to his gaze.

Jason thought he'd never seen anything as erotic or beautiful as the sight of Caroline Banks, spread naked across his bed with her knees bent. She stole his breath. Her feminine folds enticed him from beneath a narrow strip of curls.

"Oh, man," he groaned. "You are so incredibly, amazingly perfect." He cupped her with one hand. Her skin was like hot silk. When he parted her and slid a finger along her slick cleft, she cried out and arched against his hand.

"I need you," she said, "inside me."

He grew even harder at her words. "Soon, baby," he promised. "There's just something I have to do first."

Pushing himself backward, he knelt on the floor by the edge of the bed and slid his hands beneath her buttocks. He devoured the sight of her, pink and plump and glistening with arousal, before trailing kisses along her inner thigh. She trembled beneath his touch. When he reached her core, he breathed in her scent and then pressed a kiss directly to her center. She bucked and cried out, and her hands clutched his head.

"You taste even better than I imagined," he ground out, skating his lips along her inner thigh. "And I love how good you smell."

Jason was in heaven. Sweet, delicious heaven. He pushed her knees back as he laved her with his tongue. She made quiet noises of intense pleasure and speared her fingers through his hair. Her breath came faster and she pressed one hand against her mouth to muffle the sounds she was making. When he concentrated his efforts on the tiny bud of her clitoris and eased one finger inside her, she bowed off the mattress and her whole body tautened. Her mouth opened on a silent cry as she convulsed beneath him.

CAROLINE COULDN'T THINK. She could only lay sprawled across the bed, a helpless victim of the delicious aftershocks of what was possibly the most intense orgasm she'd ever experienced. Okay, *definitely* the most intense. Her entire body thrummed with sexual gratification. She was trembling, as weak as a kitten.

Jason eased himself down beside her and pulled her into his arms. "Good?"

"Ohmigod. Better than good. Amazing."

"I agree," he murmured and tilted her face so that he could kiss her again. Caroline returned the kiss, sliding her tongue against his in a slow, sensual mating. When she would have wound her arms around his neck, Jason caught her wrists in his hands and pinned them gently but firmly over her head. She'd known he was a big man, but it wasn't until he was over her like this, with her breasts flattened against the muscles of his chest, that she realized just how large he really was.

He smiled down at her in a way that caused something in her chest to contract. His eyes were smoldering as they raked her features. "We've only just gotten started."

He shifted against her, and she could feel the unmistakable thrust of his erection bumping against her hip. Caroline's breath hitched. She liked this side of Jason, sexy and masculine. The heat she saw in his eyes made her feel uninhibited and completely desirable. At sixteen, she hadn't known her own power. But now she realized that what he had said was true—she had all the control. Despite the fact that he had her wrists pinned over her head, she was the one who was calling the shots.

"Maybe this time," she murmured, her gaze fastened on his delectable mouth, "we can finally finish what we started all those years ago."

"I'm counting on it."

He released her wrists and Caroline slid a hand up over his chest to his shoulder. She wanted to touch him everywhere. His skin was like hot satin beneath her fingers. Hooking a leg over his thigh, she pressed intimately against him, reveling in the feel of him, hard and pulsing, against the juncture of her thighs. She slid a hand between their bodies and cupped him through the stretchy material of his briefs, loving how he jerked beneath her fingers.

"Oh, my," she murmured appreciatively, then slipped her fingers beneath the waistband to take him in her hand, dragging a little grunt from him. He felt incredible in her palm. She stroked her thumb over the head of his erection, feeling the slick moisture there.

"I think you have too many clothes on," she whispered, pressing her lips against his chest. "Can we do something about that?"

"You bet." His response was immediate; he pushed both his jeans and his briefs off and kicked them free. And there he was, rising thick and rigid against the flatness of his stomach. Caroline's mouth went dry as she thought of that part of him inside her.

She dragged her gaze upward, forcing herself to look into his eyes. They were as green as the surf that pounded the sands outside and turbulent with passion. For her. A primal thrill coursed through her at the look of raw desire on his face.

"Hurry," she urged.

He took her hand and guided it back to him, and Caroline needed no further incentive to wrap her fingers around him. He pulsed strongly against her palm. God, he was so hot. And hard. And satiny beneath her fingertips.

She slid her hand down the length of his shaft and felt a rush of possessive pride when he sucked his breath in sharply and then buried his face against her neck. Caroline continued to stroke him, tentatively at first and then with growing confidence as he groaned softly and bent his head to her breast, capturing her nipple in his mouth and drawing deeply on it.

And there it was again. The slow, throbbing ache that made her long to wrap her legs around him and bring him completely inside her.

"Jason," she whispered against his hair, "please..."

He raised his head from her breast, and his eyes were startlingly bright, as if lit from within. "Yeah?"

"I want you. Inside me."

Without a word, he reached over the edge of the bed to fumble with his discarded jeans. When he came back, he held a small foil package.

A condom! God, she hadn't even thought about protection. She was grateful that Jason still had the ability to think rationally, and she wondered how often he found himself in this kind of situation. Did he always carry a condom in his pocket, or had he come prepared specifically because he was hoping to hook up with her? She found she didn't really care which it was. She had dreamed of this moment, and now that it was really happening, she didn't want to worry too much about his motives.

She watched as he covered himself and then positioned himself above her. Reaching down, he lifted one of her legs and laid it across his back, opening her. He stroked a finger along the seam of her sex, and Caroline gasped at the exquisite sensation. Pleasure lashed through her. When she felt the smooth knob of his erection nudging against her, she lifted her hips in invitation.

"Do you want me to stop?" His voice was rough, his breathing coming in pants. His gaze didn't waver as he stared down at her.

"No. Please, no."

With his eyes fixed on hers, he surged forward in one powerful thrust and sank himself fully in her heat. His possession of her was so total, so complete, that she almost stopped breathing.

"Oh, God," she whispered and closed her eyes.

"Look at me," he ground out.

Caroline opened her eyes. He braced himself above her, his eyes glittering with masculine satisfaction. He didn't move, just let her adjust to him. "Doing okay?"

"Oh, yeah," she murmured. "You feel incredible. I don't want you to hold back, Jason."

She didn't want him treating her with kid gloves. She wanted all of him—all his passion—without any restraints. She shifted her hips experimentally beneath him, and the slide of his flesh against hers was almost too wonderful to bear.

Jason closed his eyes briefly, as if in pain. "This feels too good. I'll try to go gently, but goddamn, you're so snug."

Then, with their gazes locked on each other, he began to move, pumping slow and deep. Each new stroke heightened her sensitivity, and she could feel her inner muscles clench greedily around his hard length. This is what she had wanted—what she had waited for.

Jason. Making love to her.

Caroline gasped as he filled her, and she clutched feverishly at his shoulders. He captured her mouth with his, sweeping his tongue against hers. His big hands cupped her buttocks and lifted her to better meet the bone-melting thrusts of his hips against hers. She arched against him and raised both legs to wrap them around his lean hips.

"That's it," he murmured against her mouth. "Just let go."

Caroline had never felt anything so all-consuming. He filled her, surrounded her and drove out every conscious thought she had. There was only him, connected to her.

She was being swept upward in a vortex of sensations, mindless to everything but the fierceness of her need. He was moving faster now, pumping into her with increasing urgency. He lifted his head to look at her. His features were taut, and a vein pulsed in his neck. He was close to climaxing, and knowing that she was responsible was a powerful aphrodisiac. Liquid heat flooded to the spot where he stroked her and heightened the sharpness of her desire.

"Jason," she breathed as she felt her own orgasm building again, even more intense than before.

He smoothed the damp tendrils of her hair back from her face. "I'm here," he said huskily. "I'm right here with you, babe." He adjusted the angle of his hips against hers, so that each stroke ground him against her clitoris. He thrust deeper until he filled her completely. "I want you to come again."

His words pushed her over the edge.

"Oh, oh," Caroline gasped, and Jason caught her small, frantic cries with his mouth, spearing his tongue against hers as he moved faster, pushing her higher with each mind-shattering drive of his hips.

She climaxed in a blinding white-hot rush of pleasure. Jason bucked against her, and she felt him stiffen and then shudder once, twice and then again, inside her. He collapsed onto her, his heart pounding erratically, and she wrapped her arms around him, not wanting to let him go. She stroked her hands over his back, slick with sweat, and reveled in the feel of his body, heavy and replete against hers.

"Ahh...damn," he gasped. "That was unbelievable." He raised himself on his elbows over her. He kissed her, slowly and languorously, but made no move to withdraw from the warmth of her body. When he finally pulled back to look at her, his expression was intensely serious and filled with a tenderness that made her chest ache. "You okay?"

Caroline gazed at him. "I think so." Her legs were still curved around his hips, and their breathing was uneven as they stared at one another.

As if unable to help himself, Jason dipped his head and kissed her again, a kiss so sweet that she thought she could willingly stay in his arms like that forever. When he finally lifted his head, it was to carefully withdraw from her body. After rolling away from her, he sat on the edge of the bed to dispose of the condom. But he didn't immediately come back and pull her into his arms as she wanted him to.

Reaching out, she tentatively touched Jason's back. "That was even better than I could have imagined."

In the indistinct light, his expression was difficult to read. Finally, he eased himself back down beside her. Reaching down, he retrieved a quilt that lay folded at the foot of the bed, opened it and covered them both with it. Pulling her against his side, he smoothed her hair back behind her ear and gently ran the back of his knuckles across her cheek.

"This is definitely going to complicate things," he said wryly, but he took the sting out of his words by dropping a kiss onto the corner of her mouth.

"It's what I wanted," Caroline assured him.

"Like I said…spoiled rotten."

This time there was no malice in his words, and she smiled up at him. "You'd do better to remember that I always get what I want."

He was silent for a moment. "You should want more than what I can offer."

Raising herself on one elbow, Caroline studied his face in the darkness. "I've done a lot of growing up in the last twelve years," she finally said. "And while I may not have as much experience with the opposite sex as you have, I do have enough to know what I want."

His mouth curved in a rueful smile. "Just tell me you didn't make good on your promise to have a dozen other guys when you were only sixteen."

His tone was teasing, but Caroline could hear the underlying question in his voice.

"There've been a few," she acknowledged, thinking of her past relationships. "But not until I was in college, and not even close to a dozen."

"I'm glad to hear it."

"I have no regrets, Jason." She was glad that the darkness hid her expression. Didn't he see that she'd gotten exactly what she wanted? She knew he'd had a rough upbringing, and that maybe he had some lingering insecurities about his background, but she'd never considered him beneath her, and the inference that he was somehow unworthy of her was disturbing.

"I'm glad," he said gruffly and pulled her down beside him, so that her cheek rested on his chest. She could hear his heart beating and wondered how long this dream would last.

7

JASON NEEDED A stiff drink.

Badly.

He'd waited until Caroline had fallen asleep; then, unable to close his own eyes, he'd finally gone downstairs. Barefoot and shirtless, he strode to the wet bar and poured himself a shot of Judge Banks's best bourbon, then quaffed it in a single gulp. He gasped as the liquor burned its way down his throat and set the empty glass down on the counter.

Sex with Caroline had exceeded anything Jason could have imagined, and he'd imagined a lot. He just hadn't been prepared for how completely she'd made love with him. She hadn't held anything back, and she hadn't let him hold back, either. As much as he'd like to tell himself this was only about sex, he knew differently. Despite what she'd told him all those years ago, Caroline wasn't the kind of woman to sleep with a guy unless it meant something to her, and that was causing him all kinds of guilt.

With a groan, he scrubbed his hands over his face and sat down at the table where he had spread out the case files. After several moments, he gave up any pretense of looking at the documents. He couldn't concentrate. All he could think about was Caroline. Upstairs, in his bed.

Naked.

He could still taste her, still feel the satiny texture of her skin beneath his fingertips. Still hear the feminine sounds of pleasure she'd made as he'd brought her to orgasm. He didn't think he'd ever experienced anything as sexy and beautiful as Caroline Banks in the throes of ecstasy.

No question about it—he was in serious trouble. If she had even an inkling of where he'd come from or what he'd done in the past, she'd never have considered inviting him into her bed. He tried not to think about what would happen if she were to see through his carefully constructed veneer, to what he really was inside.

In the next instant, he realized it didn't even matter. She wasn't staying in California, and he wasn't about to let himself get serious about her, even if she was. He thought he'd put his past behind him, but it was times like this when he realized he was still very much that angry boy from the wrong side of the tracks. Despite his personal successes, he couldn't quite convince himself that he was good enough for Caroline Banks. He had no doubt that eventually she'd come to the same realization.

With a deep sigh, he laced his fingers together behind his head and stared at the ceiling, envisioning Caroline curled up in bed. Before he could change his mind, he pushed his chair back and took the stairs two at a time.

He still believed that she deserved better than him, but he silently acknowledged that he wasn't above taking whatever she offered. He was a selfish bastard and not afraid to admit it.

Outside his bedroom, he paused, and then he carefully opened the door. It took a moment for his eyes to adjust to the darkness, but he could just make out her form under the blanket. Quietly, he shucked his jeans and slid in behind her. She gave a sleepy murmur of surprise and then shifted so her back was pressed against his chest. Groping with one hand, she found his arm and dragged it over her body so that he was wrapped around her. She was warm, and she smelled like the fragrant soap she'd used in the shower. It took all his restraint not to let his hands roam everywhere. Instead, he forced himself to remain still, but there was nothing he could do about his growing arousal.

"Where'd you go?" she whispered.

Jason leaned over and kissed her. "Just downstairs for a minute. You okay?"

She squeezed his hand and brought it up to cover one bare breast. "Better than okay. That was perfect. You were perfect. Even better than my fantasies."

Jason groaned, knowing he was a goner. Her breast was heavy and soft in his hand, and he cupped it gently, stroking his thumb over her nipple until it tightened beneath his touch. While there was a part of him that was scared shitless about what had happened between them, another part of him was filled with masculine satisfaction. For tonight, it was enough. He wouldn't let himself think about tomorrow.

JASON LEFT THE bed as the first fingers of light were touching the ocean beyond the dunes. He crept silently down the stairs, unwilling to wake her. After last night, she needed her sleep more than she needed to rush to her father's bedside. As he entered the kitchen, he stopped short.

Colton leaned against the counter with a cup of coffee in one hand and a disapproving expression on his face. Silently, he poured a second cup of coffee from the fresh pot he had brewed and handed it to Jason.

"Don't say it," Jason warned, accepting the mug.

"What were you doing upstairs?" Colton asked. "Please tell me you weren't with her."

Jason took a gulp of the hot liquid, ignoring the other man's question. "Have you been in touch with the hospital?"

Colton nodded. "Yeah. There's been no change to the judge's condition." He glanced at his watch. "What time do you want to leave?"

Jason walked over to the table and pretended to consider the files that were strewn across the surface. "I thought I'd let Caroline catch up on her sleep. She had a pretty rough day yesterday."

Colton was too well trained to comment, but Jason knew the other man wasn't fooled. The truth was, he and Caroline hadn't gotten very much sleep after he'd returned to bed. Jason was still riding an adrenaline high, but he knew he'd be feeling the effects of the strenuous night before the day was through. He was trained to go for extended periods without sleep, but Caroline wasn't. The emotional stress she was under, combined with the physical demands he'd made of her, meant she would be exhausted unless she got some rest.

"It's more difficult to be objective when you're emotionally involved with your detail," Colton commented. "Not to mention that it's not very professional. I know you and Caroline go way back, but I'm not sure this is the time or place to rediscover whatever it is you had together."

Jason shot him a baleful look. "Let it go, Black."

Colton made a sound of disgust as he pushed away from the counter and headed for the door, coffee mug in hand. "I hope you know what you're doing. I'll be outside if you need me."

Jason didn't take offense at the other man's words. The two of them had worked together for over five years, and Colton was the closest thing he had to a friend. If their positions were reversed, he'd have expressed the same concerns. He didn't regret last night, but he acknowledged that sleeping with Caroline might not have been the smartest idea. But now that he had, everything had changed.

She was his, in the most elemental way there was. He wouldn't let anything happen to her. In order to protect her, he needed to find out who had shot her father. Whoever was responsible was still out there. And while the FBI had formal jurisdiction over the case and was performing its own investigation, Jason knew it couldn't hurt for him to review the files. He had an immediate familiarity with most of the cases and a good instinct for what might have motivated such a vicious attack.

Pulling up a chair, he set his mug down and began

methodically going through the files. Steve Anderson had done him a favor by segregating the worst offenders out of the pile of possible suspects. Flipping through the documents, Jason discarded one and then another file. He set two of the files to one side, believing they warranted a closer look.

The first was the Sanchez case, and while Jason knew the leader of the drug-smuggling gang was more than capable of putting a hit out on the judge, he wasn't sure that would be his style. Sanchez would lose any hope of serving out the remainder of his prison term in Mexico if the authorities even suspected he was behind the shooting. But it was possible that one of his henchmen had acted in retaliation. He set the file aside for further investigation.

He reached for the next file, and then hesitated when he saw the name that was written across the top. He told himself that Edward Green was a common enough name, but when he opened the file, he recognized the man in the police photo. Eddie Green was one of the most notorious gang leaders in the Hunters Point region of San Francisco. He'd been charged with numerous offenses, including drug distribution, operating a prostitution ring, weapons possession and murder. Jason recognized him from his own childhood. They had grown up together in the projects, and Jason had been one of Eddie's earliest recruits into his violent Hunters Point gang.

He closed his eyes briefly against the unwelcome memories. He'd been twelve years old to Eddie's sixteen, and he had worshipped the older boy, for both his cunning and his reckless attitude. Eddie Green didn't take crap from anyone, and if someone did him wrong, he meted out his own form of brutal punishment. When he was seventeen, he'd been suspected of beating his mother's boyfriend to death, but no charges had ever been pressed.

Jason couldn't think about those days without a degree of self-loathing. He'd had a crummy homelife, with a grandmother who worked too much to really be an influence in his life and a father who was a drug addict. His grandmother had died when he was fifteen, and after that, Daryl Cooper had been too concerned about where his next fix was coming from to worry about what illegal activities his kid might be involved in. Jason had never known his mother. She'd been gone long before he was old enough to remember her. Eddie Green and his budding gang had seemed like family to Jason, and he'd looked up to Eddie as he would have an older brother.

Even when Eddie had demanded he commit petty crimes in order to prove his loyalty and commitment to the gang, Jason hadn't stopped hanging out with the group. He'd deluded himself into thinking that it was okay to rob a convenience store or break into someone's home when they weren't there and steal their jewelry and electronics. He'd told himself that society owed him something for dealing him such a lousy hand. Still, on some level, he knew it was only a matter of time before he'd be told to kill someone. But by then he was too deeply entrenched to get out. Then his grandmother had died, and Jason had realized that if he didn't extricate himself, he was going to end up dead or a junkie like his father. He'd been arrested three days later for jacking a car and had ended up in Judge Banks's courtroom.

Looking back, it was the best thing that could have happened to him.

He flipped through Eddie's file, noting that his former friend had been released from prison about fourteen months earlier, having served six years on a murder conviction. But Eddie's younger brother, Mikey, along with another key gang member, were on death row, charged in the murder of two police officers. Eddie's gang had threatened to take down everyone involved in the sentencing if Mikey's conviction wasn't overturned. Judge Banks had been the one who had sentenced the two men.

Closing the file, Jason sat back in his chair, feeling as if he'd had the wind knocked out of him. He knew what Eddie and his men were capable of. They were ruthless criminals without consciences, and they would absolutely destroy anyone who got in their way. But would they go so far as to shoot a superior court judge in his own home? Jason didn't know. He thought again of what Steven Anderson had said about seeing an old car parked in the Sea Cliff neighborhood, conspicuous because of its age and condition. Could it have been Eddie, or one of his gang members, in that car? Just thinking about that scumbag coming anywhere near Caroline made his blood run cold.

Jason no longer identified with the troubled youth he'd once been, and he'd done his best to put his past behind him. But there were times, like now, when the memories of his upbringing clung to him like a dirty second skin that no amount of washing could remove. As much as the idea repulsed him, he knew he'd have to return to Hunters Point and get whatever information he could about Eddie Green and Judge Banks.

He looked up when he heard footsteps on the stairs and saw Caroline slowly making her way toward him. She wore his discarded T-shirt and a pair of shorts, and she hadn't bothered brushing her hair. She looked so sexy that Jason felt his heart thud in his chest.

"Good morning," he murmured, rising to his feet. "Did you sleep okay?"

She nodded and moved into his arms as naturally as if they'd been lovers for years. She was warm and supple and she smelled good enough to eat. Jason closed his eyes and hugged her tightly, unable to believe that this woman wanted to be with him.

"I missed you when I woke up," she said and pressed a kiss against his jaw.

"I wanted to let you sleep, and it gave me time to start going through these case files."

Caroline inspected the open file on the table. Jason wanted to slap it shut and prevent her from reading about the sordid details of Eddie Green's history.

"I remember overhearing my father talking about this guy when I was a kid," she said, picking up the photo of Eddie and inspecting it. "He sure is a scary-looking guy."

Standing behind her, Jason studied the photo she held in her hand. Eddie had changed in the years since Jason had known him. He'd shaved his head, and the exposed skin was covered with intricate tattoos that extended down his neck and over his shoulders and chest. He had gauges in both ears and a piercing in one eyebrow, but it was none of these things that made him look frightening. It was the utter deadness of his eyes.

"He lost his way a long time ago," Jason said.

Caroline replaced the photo in the file and picked up the written report, scanning quickly through Eddie's rap sheet.

"He's one nasty character." She turned and looked at him. "He's from Hunters Point, too. Did you know this guy?"

"I'd rather not talk about it." He didn't want to share his troubled youth with Caroline. He'd worked hard to put it behind him. He'd dedicated his life to putting creeps like Eddie Green behind bars. He didn't want her to even think of him and Eddie in the same thought. "Like you said, he's a bad character."

She reached up and gently traced one of the scars on his face with her fingertip. "I remember when this was brand-new," she said. "You had so many scars back then. I asked my father about them once, but he wouldn't tell me anything."

"Because he wanted to keep that ugliness out of your life," he said, brushing a strand of hair back from her face. "You were so young and so damned sweet. I'm still surprised that he even let me into his house, considering what he knew of me."

"Because he has a unique ability to see the true character of people," she said, rubbing her finger over his lower lip. "He knew that you were a good person. Just like I knew."

Her words grabbed hold of something in his chest and squeezed hard, making it difficult for him to breathe.

She's not yours to keep. He told himself again that this was only temporary, and he'd do better if he remembered that. Caroline Banks would never commit herself to a guy like him, at least not permanently. But it was difficult to think straight when she pressed her mouth against his and kissed him slowly and languorously. Her lips were soft, and she tasted faintly of toothpaste. For just a moment, Jason resisted. But his body had other ideas, and before he could prevent himself, he slid his hands into her hair and tilted her face, fitting his mouth over hers. He pushed her back against the table before cupping her rear in his hands and lifting her onto the surface, heedless of the papers that went scattering.

He swallowed Caroline's surprised gurgle of laughter and situated himself between her thighs, pressing forward until she couldn't help but feel his growing arousal. Her laughter died, and she deepened the kiss, clutching him with a new intensity. Jason knew they couldn't do this now.

Reluctantly, he broke the kiss, smoothing his thumb along the clean line of her jaw. "We should probably head back to San Francisco."

Caroline nodded and rolled her lips inward, as if she could still taste him. "Okay. Give me fifteen minutes, and I'll be ready to go."

"I'll make us something to eat while you shower," he offered and lifted her from the table.

"Someday," Caroline stated, glancing at Eddie's file, "you'll tell me about your past and how you got those scars."

Jason tried to keep his tone light. "Don't count on it."

Leaning up, she kissed him briefly. "Oh, but I will. You won't stand a chance."

After she left, Jason sighed, knowing she was right.

He didn't stand a chance. While he might want two un-
interrupted weeks with her in the bedroom upstairs, now
wasn't the time. But he promised himself that when this
was all over, and if Caroline was still interested in him,
they'd find a quiet place to hole up and get to know each
other better. He just hoped when they did, she wouldn't
be disappointed with what she discovered.

8

CAROLINE SAT NEAR her father's bed and watched his chest rise and fall. The only sounds in the room were the rhythmic whir of the ventilator as it pumped air into his chest and the steady beep of the heart monitor, reassuring her that he was still alive. She didn't know how long she'd been sitting there, willing him not to die. She only knew that she couldn't lose him.

After a moment, Caroline dropped her head into her hands. Why hadn't she visited him when she'd had the chance? Why had she stubbornly insisted on remaining so far away for so long? Her reasons now seemed so ridiculous and unimportant.

Let him live, and I'll come home. I'll be a better daughter. I'll make sure he knows how much I love him.

Raising her head, Caroline swiped at her damp cheeks and dragged in a deep breath. Then, setting her shoulders, she pushed herself to her feet and crossed the room to where Jason had left the box of case files on a small table in the corner. She needed to do something to stay occupied, and when she'd suggested to Jason that she could review her father's case files, he'd been more than happy to let her do that. He'd seemed to understand her need to be useful.

Sitting by her father's bedside gave her too much opportunity to think, and she didn't want to overanalyze whatever it was that she and Jason shared.

Despite the fact they'd been as intimate as two people could possibly be, and even though he'd been incredible in bed, ensuring she reached her pleasure before he found his own, he remained emotionally detached. She hadn't expected a declaration of love, but she'd thought he might have given her some indication of how he felt. But he'd been distant and preoccupied on the ride back to San Francisco. Still, she hadn't been too concerned until he'd told her that he wouldn't be staying with her at the hospital that day. Instead, he'd turned his protection detail over to Deputy Black and had left. He hadn't even given her the courtesy of an explanation or an idea of when he would return.

If Deputy Black knew where Jason was going, he didn't tell Caroline. She couldn't help but wonder if it had anything to do with her, if perhaps he'd needed some time to himself. They hadn't spoken about the previous night, although it consumed all her thoughts.

After he had returned to bed, they'd taken their time exploring each other. He had known just how to touch her, so that before long she was squirming in his arms, desperate for release. They didn't have a second condom, so he'd used his fingers and mouth to torment her and finally bring her to completion. After that, he'd let her reciprocate, and she didn't think she'd ever seen anything as erotic and thrilling as Jason Cooper losing control.

But in the morning, his law enforcement persona was firmly back in place, and he was all business. She thought about the file she had seen on the kitchen table for a career criminal named Eddie Green. She only vaguely recalled hearing stories about him when she was a teenager and wished now that she had paid closer attention. What she did know was that her father had sentenced Eddie Green's brother to death, and Eddie had promised retribution unless his brother was released. That made him a top suspect in Caroline's eyes.

She quickly examined the folders in the box and then scanned through them a second time. To her dismay, the file for Eddie Green was missing. Had Jason taken it with him? Did he believe that this man was somehow involved in her father's shooting?

And then she knew.

Jason had gone to see Eddie Green. The file had listed his address as Hunters Point, which was also where Jason had grown up. Caroline wondered if they had known each other, and recalled how Jason had deliberately shut her down when she'd asked that very question. Had their paths crossed when they had both lived in Hunters Point? It would make sense that Jason might have fallen in with Eddie as a kid, which had led to him getting into trouble.

Curious, Caroline went in search of Deputy Black and found him standing outside in the corridor, speaking into his earpiece. When he saw Caroline, he turned away from her and lowered his voice, then abruptly ended the conversation. When he turned around again, she could see the concern on his face.

"Everything okay, ma'am?"

"I don't know," she replied. "Is it?"

He narrowed his eyes, as if trying to decipher the meaning behind her words, before drawing her a little away from the door and the guard who sat outside.

"What is it?"

"Did Jason go to Hunters Point?"

His voice grew cautious. "Why would you think that?"

Caroline gave him a tolerant look. "Because he took the file on Eddie Green. I know that this guy had a thing against my father for putting some of his gang members—including his own brother—on death row, and that his last known address was Hunters Point. Is that where Jason went?"

Deputy Black's lips compressed into a thin line, and he considered her for a long moment before he spoke. "Jason knows that area well, and he knows what he's doing. He's a U.S. marshal."

"Has he even been back there since he was a kid?" Caroline demanded. "Well, has he? That place hasn't gotten any better over the years, Deputy. At least tell me that he brought backup."

Deputy Black nodded tersely. "We have support from the local P.D., and there are undercover guys tailing him. He'll be fine."

Caroline wasn't convinced, but knew she had little choice but to accept what he said. He was right; she needed to trust that Jason knew what he was doing. He might be the youngest U.S. marshal in California, but he'd been in law enforcement for over ten years. He hadn't been appointed to his position because he was afraid to take on guys like Eddie Green. He'd gotten the job because on some level, he understood men like Eddie Green. And maybe, deep down, he was even a little bit like them.

"Okay," she finally said, turning back to her father's room. "But let me know the second he returns."

Without waiting for a response, she closed the door quietly and returned to the small table where she had been working. She knew Jason wanted to evaluate every possible suspect, and she could help him with that. After sitting down, she pulled the first file from the box. She'd go through every case her father had been involved in and make her own assessments about whether or not the claimants might have had reason to hurt him. She glanced over at William, who lay unresponsive in his bed, surrounded by the sounds of the medical equipment that helped to keep him alive. Straightening her spine, she opened the first folder.

HUNTERS POINT HADN'T changed since Jason had been a teenager. Now, driving through the streets and seeing the evidence of poverty and neglect, he knew why he had never been back. There was nothing for him here. As he turned down several side streets and saw groups of inner-city youths on the street corners and congregated on the front steps of the tenement buildings, he thought that could easily have been him. That *had* been him, some twenty years earlier. He'd preferred to hang out with the older boys in the neighborhood than go to school. At least until his father had gotten a call from the principal about his absences.

Jason absently fingered the scar on his cheekbone, where his father's ring had caught the skin and laid it open. The old man had always had a hell of a backhand.

The kids watched as he drove past, and Jason knew they were looking at the distinctive U.S. Marshals insignia on the doors of the silver SUV and were taking bets on who he was after. Jason wondered how many of the youths were actually undercover police officers, trying to in-filtrate the narcotics ring that purportedly operated out of the Point.

Glancing at the computer screen of the dash-mounted laptop, where he'd keyed in the last known address of Eddie Green, he turned down another side street, this one lined with what looked like abandoned warehouses. Furtive movement in the alleyways between the buildings told him he was being watched, probably by Green's men. He also knew that Eddie and his gang members had been under surveillance by federal law enforcement for some time, and that he was likely being observed by under-cover agents. Nevertheless, he had his service revolver in his shoulder holster and another in the back of his waist-band, concealed by his sports coat. He had no illusions that he'd be allowed to keep either once he found Eddie.

Parking the SUV in front of a derelict building, he stepped out and then tipped his head back to look up toward the roof. The windows on the lower floors were boarded up, but the top floor windows were intact and even appeared to be recently installed. He definitely had the right address.

"Yo, mister, whatchya doing here? You lost?"

Jason turned to see a group of boys and young men standing near the rear of the car. There were six of them, ranging in age from about fourteen to mid-twenties. He braced his hands on his hips, pushing his jacket back just enough for them to see his badge and his gun.

"I'm here to see an old friend," he replied. "Maybe you know him? Eddie Green."

He saw the oldest man's eyes flick upward to the top floor of the building, and Jason knew he'd been right— Green lived in this building. Jason also noted how three of the other youths kept one hand loosely behind their backs, which meant they were carrying weapons in the backs of their pants. After closer inspection, he realized that two of the young men wore surveillance earpieces similar to what he wore when he was on duty. Eddie already knew he was here. The message was clear, and Jason knew they wouldn't hesitate to kill him if the ringleader decided he was a threat. Several members of their gang were already on death row for murdering a police officer. No doubt they each considered it a badge of honor, and Jason felt a little ill at the thought that he had once been like these derelicts.

"You sure about that?" the first man asked. "Last time I checked, Eddie wasn't friends with no cops."

"Yeah, I'm sure." Reaching into his back pocket, he withdrew a slim length of photos, the kind you got from a coin-operated photo booth. The black-and-white pictures were of him and Eddie and another boy, Nick, taken one summer on the boardwalk. "We go way back."

The man stepped forward and took the photos, glancing suspiciously between the pictures and Jason. Jason didn't miss how his eyes widened when he recognized the younger version of Eddie, with hair and without his signature tattoos. His eyes narrowed as he continued examining the young boy in the photo, after a while finally acknowledging it was Jason.

He looked at his companions and gave them a curt nod. "Yo, my man, watch the car. Don't let nothing happen to it." Turning to Jason, he swaggered forward and handed him the photos. "Follow me."

Jason studied him for a moment and then nodded, indicating the other man should precede him. He didn't doubt his own abilities to protect himself, but he didn't like the thought of anyone sneaking up behind him. Now he followed the man through an alleyway to a reinforced steel door. Inside, the building appeared as empty and dilapidated as the exterior would lead you to believe, but the freight elevator was in good working condition.

"Just take it to the top, man."

Jason stepped into the elevator and closed the steel grate, never taking his eye off the other man, until the elevator slid smoothly upward and the guy disappeared from sight. On the top floor, Jason opened the doors and found himself in a hallway that was garishly lit. There was only one door visible, and he could see that it was partially open.

As he walked slowly toward the door, he saw the shadows of several figures at the end of the corridor and knew that Eddie's henchmen were standing around the corner, just out of sight. He kept his hands carefully away from his own weapon and toed the door open wide enough to look inside.

"Hey, man," a voice called from inside the apartment. "C'mon in—it's all good."

Jason stepped inside. Two enormous men immediately converged on him and quickly patted him down. Having expected this, Jason didn't protest; he waited while they confiscated his two weapons and his badge. He was in a spacious loft apartment. The walls were exposed brick and beams, and the living area was richly decorated with leather furnishings and high-end stereo and electronics. However, Jason wasn't fooled by the fancy window dressing—he knew Eddie to be a hardened criminal, and everything he owned was the result of those crimes. He might like to surround himself with expensive things, but it didn't change who—or what—he was.

A state-of-the-art kitchen occupied one end of the apartment, and a man stood behind the counter, preparing what looked like breakfast. The two henchmen brought his guns and his badge over to the kitchen and dropped them onto the granite island. Eddie studied the badge for a moment and then gave a curt jerk of his chin toward the door. The men left, pushing past Jason without a word. He knew they would stand just outside the door, ready to intervene if Eddie gave them any indication.

Now he stood with his finger on the button of a blender, watching Jason. He wore a white sleeveless T-shirt and a pair of baggy workout pants. Tattoos covered his head, neck, shoulders and arms. Several gold chains hung around his neck, and two chunky rings flashed on his right hand.

For an instant, Jason could actually feel his own tattoos burning into his skin. His grandmother had been
so disappointed when she'd first seen them, Jason had
felt some remorse. But back then, impressing Eddie had
been more important than making his grandmother proud
of him.

"Nice place you have here," Jason commented, glancing around the apartment.

"Yeah, thanks." Eddie shrugged. "The rent is cheap,
and I kinda like the neighborhood." He paused. "So what
brings a U.S. marshal out here? Alone?" He gestured
around him with one hand. "This place has been searched
at least a dozen times in the last year, and it's clean. You
won't find anything illegal here, Marshal. I'm an upstand-
ing citizen of San Francisco."

"Yeah, I'm sure you are," Jason drawled. Walking
over to where Eddie stood, he withdrew a photo of Judge
Banks and tossed it onto the counter. "I don't suppose
you recognize this man?"

Eddie's gaze flicked from Jason to the photo; then he
picked it up to study it more closely. "This is that judge
that got shot, right?" He flicked the photo back onto the
counter. "Wish I could say I'm sorry, but I got two men
on death row because of that fucker. Is the judge dead?"

Jason ignored the question. "What do you know about
the shooting?"

Eddie's eyes widened in mock surprise. "Why would I
know anything about it? Are you suggesting I had something to do with it?" He snorted. "If you knew anything
about me, you'd know that ain't how I operate."

Jason leaned over the counter and put his hand over

the judge's photo, sliding it back. "I know exactly how you operate, Eddie. I was your first recruit."

"Do I know you?" He stared at Jason for a moment, his eyes narrowing, before he gave a bark of astonished laughter. "Jesus Christ! Is that you, Cooper?"

In an instant, his entire demeanor changed. He came around the counter, his hands stretched out. "Jesus, man, you just vanished from the face of the fucking earth, and now here you are, all dressed up like a fucking cop. How you been, man?"

Jason didn't shake the other man's hand, but he didn't object when Eddie gave him a swift, hard embrace. He reeked of some expensive cologne that stayed in Jason's nostrils even after they stepped apart.

"I've been okay," he replied stiffly. "But Judge Banks is a friend of mine. Somebody shot him on his own front steps, and I intend to find out who."

Eddie frowned, staring at Jason with an affronted expression. "And you're pointing the finger at me? Man, I am highly offended by that. It really grieves me to have you believe I would do something so cold-blooded."

"Not you, Eddie. Your boys. Like you said, Judge Banks sent two of your men to death row. That's gotta hurt."

Eddie sniffed and looked away. "Yeah. One of them is my baby brother. But whatever you think of me, you know I got a code of honor. I don't kill cops, women or kids." He gave Jason a sly smile. "So you see, you're safe—I protect the weak."

Jason ignored the insult. "What do you hear on the

street? If it wasn't your boys, you must know who was responsible."

Eddie shrugged. "I don't hear anything, at least not about the judge. But I saw on the news that he has a real pretty daughter." His expression grew sly. "I saw you on the news, too, all protective and shit, carrying her out of the house. I'll bet that uniform gets you all kinds of nice perks, huh? You banging the judge's daughter?"

Jason had to put a choke hold on his gut reaction to Eddie's crude suggestion. He wanted to smash the other's man mouth, but instead he ignored the gibe and kept his expression carefully neutral.

He had tried to shield Caroline from the television crew that had lined the street in front of her father's Sea Cliff house, but there'd been no way to avoid the cameras after she'd fainted in his arms. He'd had to carry her back to the waiting SUV, and the reporters had eaten it up, capturing the footage on film. The last thing Jason wanted was Eddie Green expressing any kind of interest in Caroline. He regretted that Eddie knew she even existed. But he realized the damage had been done, and all he could do now was downplay it and hopefully divert Green's interest elsewhere.

"What about Sanchez's men?" he asked. "I hear they've moved into your neighborhood. That can't be good for business."

He watched as Eddie's hand curled into a fist, and then he abruptly turned around and busied himself cooking breakfast. "Yeah," he threw over his shoulder. "What about Sanchez's men? Why don't you ask them about it? Them sons of bitches been bringing down the real estate value around here. Someone needs to put a stop to their illegal activities. I hope you intend to pay them a visit while you're in the area."

"Maybe."

"You want me to find out if they was involved?" he asked.

Jason knew what that would entail, and he didn't want anyone getting hurt. Eddie's form of interrogation could be deadly. "No, thanks. I've got it covered."

"Sure. Whatever." He turned around and leaned back against the counter. "So look at you. The last time I saw you, you were just a kid. You got picked up for breaking and entering, right?"

"Car theft, actually."

"And now you're a damned cop. Unbelievable. You never came back after they hauled you in. What happened to you? My boys said you went to juvie."

"Yeah, something like that." Jason didn't want to talk about himself, especially not to Eddie. After the carjacking incident, he'd ended up in Judge Banks's courtroom. The sentencing had involved sending him to a residential school for at-risk youth. At first he'd been resistant, but it hadn't been long before he'd understood that he'd been given a second chance. Judge Banks had made that possible.

"You still see your old man? I hear he's living over on Griffith, at one of them treatment centers. He must be so proud of you."

Jason hadn't seen his father in over twelve years. The last he knew, his father had been unemployed, subsisting on welfare and had been in and out of rehab.

"I don't see my father anymore," he said shortly. "Thanks for your time."

"Yeah, you take care." Eddie's mouth twisted in a semblance of a smile. "It was good seeing you, man. I mean that sincerely. And I'm glad you've done good. I mean, who knows where you'd be if you'd hung with me, right?" He gestured toward his surroundings. "Maybe if things had gone differently—if you hadn't been pinched jacking that car—you'd be the one living here."

Jason withdrew a card from his wallet and handed it to the gang leader. "Here's my number." He paused. "I know you have no reason to want to help me, but—"

"It's cool," Eddie said, taking the card. "I'll keep my ears open."

He slid Jason's badge back toward him, and then scooped up his two guns. "My boys will walk you out. Sure hate for anything to happen to a U.S. marshal right outside my front door."

Jason arched an eyebrow and fastened his badge to his belt, then followed Eddie's men back to his SUV. It took a moment before he turned on the ignition, however. His heart was pounding, and his old associate's words reverberated in his head.

If things had gone differently...

Jason squeezed the bridge of his nose, unwilling to picture himself like Eddie. He pushed aside the unwelcome memories that his visit had stirred up, reminding himself that he'd chosen a different path. He and the gang leader were like opposite sides of the same coin; they'd been punched from the same piece of metal but had been stamped with different dies.

After a moment, Jason switched on the ignition. Glancing up at the top floor of the warehouse, he could see Eddie watching him through the windows. Thrusting the SUV into gear, he slowly drove away.

As he drove away from the seedy neighborhood, he couldn't prevent himself from taking a detour down Griffith Street. He didn't want to see his father; he didn't want to see the squalor and poverty in which he was surely living. He told himself again that his old man had made his own choices and was ultimately responsible for where he was in life. But another part of him wanted to make sure that he was okay.

He drove slowly down Griffith Street, until he came to the treatment center that Eddie had mentioned. It was a modest two-story structure with an enormous, wraparound porch. Several people sat outside, watching the traffic go by. There were two old, frail-looking men sitting in chairs, smoking cigarettes. As Jason drove past, he thought one of them might be his father. But without stopping for a closer look, he couldn't be certain.

He continued down the road, telling himself he couldn't stop. Nothing good would come of seeing him face-to-face. It had taken him years to set aside the anger and resentment he'd held toward his old man. Even now, knowing that addiction was a disease and that his father was as much a victim as he was, he didn't trust himself to speak to Daryl Cooper. He didn't need that kind of disappointment in his life.

Instead, he scribbled down the name of the center, knowing that he'd make a phone call later on to determine if his father was staying there. Then he'd probably provide them with a substantial donation in which to better feed and clothe their clients. He knew the gesture would only go so far in assuaging his own guilt, but he had no desire to establish any closer reunion with his father. He had nothing to say to him, and the man had lost the right to be his father a long, long time ago. Jason would ensure he was taken care of, out of respect for his grandmother's memory, but that was it.

He didn't know if Eddie had told him the truth when he'd said he had nothing to do with the shooting. But he wouldn't take him at his word. Guys like Green had learned to survive through deception. If he hadn't been involved, Jason knew he'd piqued Eddie's interest in the case. He also knew that the gang leader liked to perceive himself as having connections, especially if those connections were with law enforcement. He might even be thinking that if he did Jason a solid, he could one day call in the favor.

Glancing at his watch, he saw he'd been gone for almost two hours. He wished now that he'd kept the room at the Fairmont. After visiting Hunters Point, he felt like he needed a shower. The smell of Eddie's cologne still clung to him. In a moment of panic, he angled the rearview mirror so that he could see his own reflection. Outwardly, he looked exactly the same, but Jason didn't feel reassured. Anyone who looked closely enough would see him for what he really was.

9

Caroline looked up as Jason entered the hospital room. She had to resist the urge to fly into his arms, she was so happy to see him.

"Are you okay?" he asked.

Caroline nodded. "Yes. Did Deputy Black tell you the good news?" She looked back at her father. "He came out of the coma this afternoon and responded to the doctors."

Jason came to stand beside her, gently squeezing her shoulder as they both looked down at the judge. "That's great."

Reaching up, Caroline covered his hand with her own. "He's not out of the woods yet, and he still has a long way to go, but the doctors are optimistic that he didn't suffer any serious brain damage."

She heard Jason exhale a long sigh of relief. More than anything, she wanted him to wrap her in his arms and tell her that everything would be okay, but she knew that he wouldn't display any overt affection toward her in public, at least not while he was officially assigned to protect her. So she contented herself with this small contact and leaned back against him.

"He's the strongest man I know," Jason murmured in her ear. "If anyone can pull through, he can."

"I agree," she said softly. "They sedated him, but the doctors think they can move him out of intensive care in a day or so."

"They didn't remove his ventilator," Jason observed.

"No." Caroline knew he was hoping that the judge would be able to identify the shooter, enabling the FBI to make an arrest. "He only opened his eyes briefly, and he was able to squeeze the doctor's hand on command. But he won't be able to speak until the ventilator is removed. Then they gave him something for the pain, which pretty much knocked him out again."

"Okay. Maybe in a day or two, he'll be able to give us an indication of who did this to him."

"I hope so," she said. "But the doctors cautioned us that he may not have any memories of that night."

They'd told Caroline and Agent Black that it wasn't uncommon for victims to have no recollection of a traumatic event.

"I guess we'll just have to wait," Jason said.

"You went out to Hunters Point," she ventured. "Did you see Eddie Green?"

Caroline thought he might deny that he'd gone out to his old neighborhood to confront the criminal, but he didn't. Instead, he drew her away from the bedside.

"I saw Eddie," he confirmed. "He said he had nothing to do with the shooting, but there's no way to really know. The ballistics came back on the bullets, but we don't have a weapon. The FBI said they only have a partial foot-print from the flower bed, and there's not enough detail to know if it belongs to the gardener or somebody else."

"So, essentially, we still don't know anything," Caroline said, unable to keep the disappointment out of her voice.

"Hey," Jason said and pulled her into his arms for a brief, hard hug. "Your dad is improving. Let's focus on that for now, okay?"

She nodded, absorbing his warmth and strength. He was right; she needed to focus on the positive. When he finally drew away, she missed the contact.

"If you're satisfied that your father is okay for a couple of hours, there's something I want to do with you this afternoon," he said carefully.

Her imagination immediately filled with erotic images of the two of them. She hadn't been able to stop thinking about the previous night and acknowledged that she desperately wanted to be alone with Jason again. To make love to him again.

"What is it?" Her voice came out a little breathless.

"I want to take you to a shooting range."

Whatever Caroline had expected, it wasn't that. She gave a bark of disbelieving laughter. "Why? If you think I'm going to even touch a gun, never mind shoot it, you're wrong."

"I'd feel better if you knew how to handle a weapon," he said seriously.

Caroline stared at him. "You're not kidding."

"There's a range not far from here. We'll spend three hours or so there today, and again tomorrow."

Something in his expression caused a frisson of uneasiness to feather its way along her spine. "Do you really think I'm in danger?"

"As I said before, the likelihood that anyone is going to target you is slim, but I'm not taking any chances. I want you familiar with how to handle a gun."

Caroline drew in a deep breath and then nodded. "Okay, fine. But I didn't really dress for a shooting range. Am I okay in what I'm wearing?"

What she was wearing was a sleeveless top in a clingy material that left her arms and shoulders bare. She'd paired it with skinny jeans and a pair of flat shoes. The outfit wasn't anything that anyone could call sexy, but when she looked at Jason, his eyes reflected masculine appreciation.

"Yeah," he finally said. "What you're wearing is great."

Feeling pleased and a little flushed by his obvious admiration, Caroline scooped up her handbag, then returned briefly to her father's bedside. "Since he's heavily sedated, the doctors said he won't regain consciousness again for a while. So I guess I'm as ready as I'll ever be."

The indoor shooting range was less than a thirty-minute drive from the hospital, and, although Caroline felt completely out of her element, Jason clearly knew what he was doing. Inside, he registered them both and procured three different handguns and enough ammunition to take down a small army. Her eyes widened when she saw the small arsenal that he carried.

"Three guns?" she asked in disbelief. "I can only shoot one at a time."

"Each one is a little different," he explained. "I want

to see which one you're most comfortable handling, and that's the one I'll get for you to keep."

Then he led Caroline to a small room, where they watched an instruction video about guns and the safe handling of them.

"Those are the basics," Jason said when the video ended. "Now we'll go to the range, and you can test your skills."

The range consisted of a series of cubicles that overlooked long, enclosed alleys. At the end of each alley was a target. From where she stood, the target looked ridiculously far away. She'd never be able to hit it.

She stood quietly while Jason fitted her with a pair of ear protectors and safety glasses.

"Safety first," he said, after he donned his own protective gear. He laid the guns and the ammunition out in front of her. "Let's start with the smallest gun."

He demonstrated how the gun worked, letting her handle it and having her load and unload the rounds from the chamber until he was satisfied she could do it without fumbling.

"When you pick up your gun," he cautioned, "always keep your finger on the outside of the trigger guard, here. Always keep your gun angled downward, and never point it at anyone unless you mean business."

Caroline did as he instructed, unprepared when he came to stand directly behind her. He was so close that her back was pressed against his brawny chest. "Okay," he said, his face close to hers. "Hold your weapon in the firing-ready position, like this."

His arms came around her, and his hands closed over

hers, showing her how to curl her fingers securely around the grip.

"Good," he approved. "Now, hold the gun tightly. When your hand begins to shake, relax your grip just a bit."

Caroline bit her lip, focusing on his instructions. "Like this?"

"Perfect. Take your other hand and hold it like this." He adjusted her left hand around the other side of the gun, aligning her thumbs to point downrange. "Your left hand is used to keep the gun steady. Don't grip the gun with it."

Caroline hitched in a breath. She was finding it difficult to concentrate when she could feel his hard body pressed up against her. He'd disapprove of her wayward thoughts, so she kept quiet, but she couldn't keep her imagination from conjuring up images of just what he could be doing while he was standing behind her.

"Now, make sure both your thumbs are clear of the hammer," he said, indicating the lever above her fingers. "When this thing pops back, it could hurt you if your hands aren't properly positioned."

Caroline nodded to let him know she understood.

"It's important to stand in the proper firing stance," he said. He stepped briefly away from her to demonstrate the stance. "Like this."

"Okay, I think I've got it," she replied.

Jason stood behind her again, and when she planted her feet, he used his own foot to widen her stance a bit more. "That's good," he said, and then he put one hand on her stomach and the other on her back and eased her forward. "You should be leaning forward just a bit," he explained. "Like this, knees slightly bent, right arm locked."

This new position put her butt into direct contact with his hips, although he seemed not to notice. He was so intent on ensuring she had the correct stance. There was definitely something wrong with her, she decided, since all she could seem to think about was sex. She could smell him. His arms were around her, and his breath was warm on her neck.

"You're doing great," he said. "Now you're going to sight the target. The two sights should be level and centered. Focus on the center of the target. Good job. Now insert your finger into the trigger guard. Try to time your firing with your breathing. Take a breath, exhale halfway and then slowly squeeze the trigger."

Caroline did as he instructed, startled by the first shot and unprepared for the recoil. She staggered a little, but Jason was right there, steadying her.

Yanking off her ear protectors, she whirled around, jubilant. Jason's eyes widened, and he reached for the weapon, redirecting it away from his midsection and back toward downrange.

"Whoa! Always know where your gun is aimed," he said, but he grinned at her. "Good job. Let's clear the rounds and do it again."

Her hand flew to her mouth as she realized she had swung the gun around and had pointed it directly at him. "Oh, my God," she breathed in horror. "I'm sorry!"

"Beginner's mistake." He shrugged. "My fault. Ready to go again?"

Caroline saw that her hands were shaking, but she

nodded and turned determinedly back toward the range, repositioning her earmuffs and goggles before she picked up the gun. But her mind was reeling with the knowledge that she could easily have shot Jason. She adjusted her stance and tried to align her sights, but all she could see was Jason, lying on the ground...bleeding.

Suddenly, his arms were around her, his fingers prying the weapon from hands that visibly shook. He laid the gun down and turned her around to face him. His expression was filled with concern, and he quickly pulled her ear protectors and goggles off.

"Are you okay?" he asked.

She shook her head and swallowed convulsively, unable to dispel the image she'd had of him. "I almost killed you."

He looked confused, and then understanding dawned. "No, sweetheart, you didn't. You made a small error, but nothing happened. Look at me...I'm fine."

Seeing her distress, he laughed softly and pulled her into his arms. "Okay, come here. It's okay, we don't have to do this. I'm probably being overprotective anyway. Nothing is going to happen to you, because I'm going to be right here."

Caroline dragged in a deep breath and pulled free of his embrace. "No, I want to finish. You might not always be here, and I want to be able to take care of myself."

Slowly, Jason smiled, and she saw the grudging admiration in his eyes. "Okay, good. Let's continue."

She put her goggles and ear protectors back on and turned determinedly back to the weapons. This time, she wouldn't let his proximity distract her. She knew how serious this was, and as she fixed her sights on the distant target, she made herself remember the blood on her father's front porch. She thought again of how frail and vulnerable he'd looked in the hospital and imagined the target was the shooter, coming back to finish the job. She fired off six shots in quick succession. When she had emptied the chamber, she set the gun down and removed the headpiece.

"Great job," Jason said. When she turned to look at him, he was grinning broadly. "Let's take a closer look."

He pressed a small button on the wall, and they watched as the target slid toward them. Even before it reached the window where they stood, she could see she had hit the center. Jason pulled the paper free from the clips, and they examined it together.

"You got four hits," he said. "All of them center mass."

Caroline studied the tiny holes. They were all within the targeted circles. "So I did good?"

"You did better than good—you did great."

"I want to go again," she said, a little astonished at the thrill of power she felt. "I don't want to stop until I hit the mark."

"Not everyone is able to hit the dead center," he cautioned. "But we can come back as many times as you want until you can."

"I'm going to do it today."

He didn't argue, simply nodded and replaced the target with a fresh sheet. They spent another hour at the range, during which Caroline practiced using each of the weapons that Jason had selected. By the end of the session, her shoulders and arms ached with the effort of handling the guns and she had a knot of tension between her eyes.

She watched as Jason gathered up the guns, handling them with an ease and familiarity that bespoke years of experience. She waited while he turned the weapons and equipment back in, and then they walked outside and climbed into the SUV.

She watched as he put the vehicle into gear, admiring the shape and strength of his hands. As if sensing her scrutiny, he glanced over at her and smiled and then reached over to cover her hand with his.

"You did great," he said. "Don't worry that you couldn't hit dead center. Like I said, sometimes it takes years to achieve that kind of marksmanship. What you did today was incredible, and I certainly wouldn't want you pointing a weapon at me."

His words brought back that horrific moment when she had inadvertently swung the gun in his direction. "Don't remind me." She cringed. "God, when I think that I could have shot you."

"But you didn't," he said. "We'll come back again, until handling a weapon becomes second nature, okay? We'll get you a weapon of your own before the end of the week, along with a license to carry."

Caroline nodded her agreement. Less than a week ago, she'd never have believed she'd be the kind of woman who would carry a concealed weapon. But that was before someone had gunned down her father. Before her life had been turned upside down.

She glanced over at Jason as he negotiated the busy city traffic, and she couldn't help but recall how good it had felt to have him standing behind her—both figuratively and literally—while she learned to shoot. But while having her own weapon, and the skill to use it, might make her feel safe, she knew there weren't enough bullets in the world to protect her heart from Jason Cooper. He'd already struck her dead center.

10

"I HAVE TO make some phone calls," Jason said when they'd returned to the hospital and she had reassured herself that her father was still resting comfortably. "You'll be okay while I'm gone? I'll try to be quick, and then maybe we can grab a bite to eat downstairs."

Caroline nodded. "That sounds good." He had turned away before she remembered that she had other news for him, which she'd almost forgotten about in the excitement over her father's condition and the shooting range. "Oh, wait."

Jason pivoted back around, his green eyes flickering with interest.

Caroline moved to the table and picked up several of the case files. "While you were gone this morning, I went through some of the cases my father was working on, and I think these three warrant a second look."

She held the files out to Jason, who took them and quickly scanned the contents. "These are medical mal-practice cases," he said.

"Well, two of them are. The third file involves Conrad Kelly, the guy who bombed all those federal buildings." Seeing his expression, she held up a hand to forestall him. "I know what you're thinking—Conrad Kelly is already serving a thirty-year sentence for the bombings, so there's no way he could have been the shooter. But he has a lot of crazy followers, Jason. What if one of them decided to get revenge on my father for the sentence?"

"Okay, I'll take a look at them as soon as I get back." Jason set the files back on the table and took Caroline by the upper arms. The touch of his fingers sent a shiver of awareness through her. When he fixed his gaze on her mouth and swallowed hard, she knew he wasn't immune to the contact, either. She could sense the effort it took for him to pull his thoughts back to their conversation. "We'll follow every lead—I promise. We'll find whoever did this."

After he left, she opened the top file. The medical malpractice case had involved a botched kidney transplant between two siblings. A young woman had been in the final stages of renal failure, and her brother had offered up one of his own kidneys. He was a perfect match, and the organ transplant would have saved his sister's life. Instead, the harvested organ had accidentally been thrown into the trash and damaged so badly that doctors had been unable to use it for the transplant. The woman had been forced to remain on dialysis until another kidney could be found, and she had passed away before that happened.

Caroline didn't understand all the nuances of the final ruling, but the hospital had received what equated to a slap on the wrist, and the family had not received any compensation for their loss.

Just reading the case made Caroline angry on behalf of the woman and her brother, so how must the family feel? Would the woman's brother be angry enough to seek revenge on her father? People went to extremes for lesser reasons, which was why she had set the file aside for further scrutiny.

The second malpractice case involved a young woman who had been admitted to the hospital with severe stomach pains. The doctors had diagnosed a ruptured appendix and had performed emergency surgery. During the procedure, the woman had gone into cardiac arrest on the operating table and had actually died. The surgeons were able to resuscitate her, but she had suffered permanent brain damage as a result. She'd survived for a week, before she had been taken off life support. An autopsy revealed she'd had an underlying, previously undiagnosed heart condition, which had been exacerbated by the anesthesia. Judge Banks had ruled in favor of the hospital.

Caroline looked over to where her father lay. He was a good judge and a good man. She knew that with all her heart. But she had a hard time believing he had ruled in favor of the hospital in both cases. Could he have made a mistake in these instances? Medical malpractice wasn't Caroline's specialty, so perhaps there were some underlying legalities that she didn't fully comprehend. But she could absolutely understand why the victims' loved ones might want to harm her father for his ruling. Nothing about it seemed fair.

At that moment, her cell phone began to vibrate in her

pocket. Pulling it out, she saw it was Patrick Dougherty, the social worker from Richmond.

"Hi, Patrick," she said.

She strained to listen, but the reception in the hotel was spotty at best, and she could only make out every third or fourth word that he said.

"Patrick," she said, interrupting his flow of words. "You're breaking up. I'm going to take the phone outside and call you right back."

Grimacing, she disconnected the call, hoping he didn't think she'd just arbitrarily hung up on him. Stepping out into the corridor, she looked for Jason, but neither he nor Deputy Black were anywhere in sight.

"Have you seen either Marshal Cooper or Deputy Black?" she asked the guard who stood vigil outside her father's door.

"Yes, ma'am," the deputy replied. "They had some calls to make but couldn't get any reception. I believe they stepped outside." He indicated the exit sign at the far end of the corridor.

"Thanks," Caroline said.

Her father's room was on the third floor of the hospital, but if she took the stairwell to the ground floor, she would be directly across from one of the main hospital entries that led to a small parking lot at the side of the hospital. Certain that was where Jason and Agent Black had gone, she made her way to the exit door.

"Ma'am?" The guard looked concerned. "I believe Marshal Cooper will be right back if you'd like to wait."

"That's okay," she demurred. "I know where to find him."

He was halfway to his feet, clearly uncertain what to do, since his own assignment was to stand guard outside the judge's hospital room. For a moment, Caroline felt sympathy for him.

"Please don't worry about me," she called. "I'll probably run into the marshal and his deputy in the stairwell."

But he was speaking into his earpiece, and Caroline pushed the door open and quickly made her way down the stairwell. On the first floor, she found herself in a wide corridor, bustling with medical personnel and visitors. Directly across from the stairwell entrance was a revolving door that led to the parking lot. Pushing through the doors, she looked around for Jason or Deputy Black, frowning when she didn't see either one of them.

It was possible they had taken the elevator back up to the third floor, in which case Jason wasn't going to be pleased to find her gone. Quickly, she redialed Patrick's number.

"Hey, Caroline," he said. "I'm glad you called me back. How's your father doing?"

"He's actually showing signs of improvement," Caroline said. "Is everything okay out there?"

"Yes, everything is fine," he assured her. "I just wanted to be sure you were okay, and to let you know that Devon Lawton was placed into a foster home. I think it's going to work out for him."

Before she could respond, a hand descended on her shoulder and spun her around. She found herself staring into Jason's face, and if his eyes had reminded her of tempered glass before, now they were positively shardlike.

"That's wonderful, Patrick. Look, I have to go," she

said hastily. "I'm sorry. I'll try to give you a call later today, okay?"

She disconnected the call, knowing her expression looked guilty.

"Let's go," Jason said. Without waiting for a response, he took her elbow in a firm grip and steered her back toward the building. At the entrance, he stiff-armed the revolving door, preventing anyone from using it, as he cleared a way for her. Then he hustled her effortlessly inside and over to the stairwell.

Only when they had climbed quickly to the third floor, and she was breathless and panting, did he finally pull her to a stop and push her up against the wall.

"Don't ever do that again," he said, his eyes blazing into hers. Then he bent his head to claim her mouth in a kiss that was both demanding and exhilarating. Pinned between his hard body and the wall, Caroline could only hang on.

Slowly, the kiss changed and became softer. Deeper.

She gave a hum of approval and slid her hands to his back, clutching him tighter. He stroked her tongue with his own, pushing past her teeth to explore her more fully. Caroline felt light-headed, but whether it was from their mad dash up the stairs or from his kiss, she couldn't tell.

Finally, he dragged his mouth away and bent his head to hers. The only sound in the stairwell was their ragged breathing. When he lifted his head to look at her, she was shocked by the expression in his eyes. He looked haunted.

"Jason." Her voice came out as a husky whisper. "What is it?"

"It's okay," he said. "I'm okay. I just didn't know where

you'd gone. And when the deputy said you'd left…" His voice trailed off.

"I'm sorry—I should have waited for you to come back, but I thought you were outside."

He gave her cheek a gentle flick of his thumb. "As if I would leave you. But Jesus, I stepped away for five minutes, and that's all it took for you to vanish."

"I'm sorry," she said again. "I just had to make a call, and I couldn't get any reception inside."

"Promise me now that you won't do that again," he said. He took the sternness out of his words by planting a warm, tender kiss against her mouth.

"I promise."

He straightened and glanced through the window of the stairwell door, to where Agent Black and the guard stood vigil outside her father's room. Caroline could see his pulse beating strongly at the base of his throat, and she realized just how much her disappearance had impacted him. The knowledge made her feel both guilty and pleased.

He exhaled harshly and scrubbed a hand over his hair. When he looked at her, she could see he was back in control. "It's almost six o'clock. Would you like to stay a bit longer or head back to Santa Cruz?"

After that smoking-hot kiss, Caroline couldn't believe he thought there was even an option. Her father was still heavily sedated and had made a turn for the better. There was nothing more she could do for him today.

"I think I'd like to head back to the beach house," she said. *As fast as you can drive, please.*

"I'll let Deputy Black know," he said, completely unaware of the direction of her thoughts. "It's getting late, and I'd like to go through those case files before it gets too late."

His words were like a dash of cold water. Caroline thought about the medical malpractice cases she had reviewed. What would Jason think about the judge's decisions in those cases? Would he agree with the rulings, or would they somehow diminish his opinion of William? Jason also had a law degree, so maybe there were nuances to the cases that he would understand. Still, there was a part of her that was reluctant for him to read the files. He'd always looked up to the judge, maybe even more than she had. She didn't want to see that change.

"Maybe the cases should wait," she said. "At least for tonight."

11

By the time they reached the beach house, it was nearly nine-thirty. They had stopped along the way for a quick bite to eat, but Caroline hadn't had much of an appetite. Jason had insisted she look at the dessert menu, and when she'd been reluctant to choose something, he'd selected two slices of chocolate cheesecake to go. They made the rest of the drive in silence, each wrapped up in their own thoughts. Behind them, on the highway, Jason could just make out Colton and Deputy Mitchell in the second car.

After parking in the gravel driveway, Jason came around and opened Caroline's door for her, before reaching into the back for the box of case files. He intended to take a look at the three cases that she thought might be linked to her father's shooting. Balancing the box under one arm, he fished in his coat pocket for the house keys, and Caroline followed him along the dark path to the front door.

"I must have forgotten to leave the front light on," she said offhandedly. "And I also forgot the cheesecake in the car. Be right back." Jason paused to watch her jog lightly back to the driveway. Deputy Black pulled in behind them, illuminating Caroline with his headlights. Satisfied that she was safe, Jason turned back to the front door and inserted the key, and then he went completely still. The door pushed open before he even turned the key.

Swiftly, he set the box down and pulled his weapon out, motioning for Colton to secure Caroline. He waited as Colton hustled her to the second car and put her in the front seat next to Deputy Mitchell, who was driving. They backed out of the driveway and drove away. Jason caught a glimpse of her pale face in the passenger window of the car before they turned a corner and disappeared from sight.

With Caroline safely out of harm's way, Jason used his foot to nudge the door open wider, holding his gun and a small flashlight out in front of him. He scoped out the room but detected no movement. Colton was at his side in seconds, his own weapon drawn, and together they did a complete sweep of the house. The rooms were empty, but whoever had broken in had trashed the place. Drawers had been pulled out and upended on the floor, and furniture and lamps had been tipped over. Picture frames and collectibles lay smashed on the floor. A quick check revealed nothing of value had been taken. The judge kept a wad of cash stashed in a drawer in the bedroom, and the contents of the drawer had been dumped out, but the money was left untouched. Whoever had broken in wasn't interested in stealing anything. They'd either hoped to find someone at home or they were sending an ominous warning.

The French doors that opened onto the balcony had been left ajar. Inspecting them, Jason saw that one of the panes of glass had been smashed, allowing the intruder to gain access.

"Okay, let's canvas the area," he said to Colton. "Check with the neighbors—see if they noticed any activity here today."

As he and Colton circled the house, Jason put in a call to the local police. He didn't know if the intruders were still in the vicinity, but he knew the extra police activity would deter them from hanging around.

Once they had cleared the perimeter of the property, he called Deputy Mitchell and let him know it was safe to bring Caroline back to the house. By the time they arrived, two cruisers were also on-site. Jason walked over to Caroline, intercepting her before she could even step onto the walkway.

"The house is clear," he said quietly, not wanting to alarm her any more than necessary. "But there's been a break-in. Someone disabled the electrical at the service drop, which is likely why the alarm wasn't triggered."

"If they wanted me, they could have waited," she pointed out in a calm voice. "But they didn't. They just wanted to scare us."

"Maybe," Jason muttered, but he knew he wasn't being truthful.

He had a pretty good sense that whoever had done this was also responsible for the shooting. The implications were frightening, and his mind raced with all the possible scenarios. Had Eddie Green been involved, after all? It seemed more than coincidence that Caroline's beach house had been tossed only hours after he had confronted Eddie.

Or was someone else responsible? One thing was certain: they were being watched. Whoever had broken into the beach house knew that they were staying there. This was a deliberate attempt to frighten them off. Instead of scaring Jason, it only pissed him off. Nobody would hurt Caroline while he was alive to prevent it. He'd protect her with every resource he had at his disposal, and no sacrifice would be too great.

"Listen, I want you to stay in the vehicle with Deputy Mitchell until I've finished talking with the police," he said, rubbing her arms. Despite the warmth of the evening, she was shivering. "We won't stay here tonight. We'll find a hotel." He gestured toward the house. "I'm just going to grab our gear, and I'll be right out. Ten minutes, tops."

"What about my father?"

"I've already taken care of it. Extra men are being assigned to protect him. Trust me—nobody is going to get within a hundred feet of the judge, okay?"

"Okay." She retreated to the cruiser, but she looked shaken and pale. "Be careful, Jason."

He crouched down on the pavement beside her open door and took her hands in his. "Whoever did this is long gone," he assured her. "This was done as a scare tactic, nothing more. That means that we're getting close to finding out who did this, and they know it. They're getting desperate."

"Which makes them more dangerous," Caroline said urgently. "Just watch your back, okay?"

"Always."

He left her under the protection of two deputy marshals while he returned to the house. Inside, the police were inspecting the damaged French doors.

"We're not going to be able to do much tonight," the lieutenant said. "We'll have to wait until the electricity is restored, or at least until tomorrow, when we have some light. We'll secure the house and leave a cruiser here overnight."

Jason nodded. "Get a team in here in the morning to dust for fingerprints, and check the area around the house for footprints, especially where the electrical input was damaged."

"Yes, sir."

Jason made his way upstairs. In Caroline's room, he gathered up her clothing from where the intruders had strewn it across the floor and bed and packed it quickly into her small suitcase. As he was leaving the bedroom, his shoes crunched over broken glass, and he bent down to inspect the floor.

He'd stepped on a picture frame. Turning it over, he saw it was a photo of Caroline and her father, taken one summer when she was just a teenager. He wanted to think that the broken picture was just collateral damage, and that the intruder hadn't deliberately smashed this particular photo. But someone had used a fat black marker to draw an *X* over both of the judge's and Caroline's eyes, reminding Jason of the stupid cartoons he used to watch as a kid. You knew when a cartoon character was dead because his eyes were crossed out. The home invasion had been personal, and if Caroline had been alone in the house, she'd likely be dead right now.

The thought chilled him.

Swiftly, he returned to his bedroom and gathered up his own discarded clothing, stuffing items into his duffel bag with no regard for whether he wrinkled them or not. He just wanted to get Caroline the hell away from the house.

It wasn't until he had her in his own car and they were speeding away from the beach house, with the flashing lights of the police cars receding in the distance, that he began to breathe easier. The car carrying Colton and Deputy Mitchell was somewhere behind them, and they'd agreed to rendezvous at a hotel about fifty miles south of San Francisco. Whoever had attacked Judge Banks had sent a clear message: they wanted Caroline, too. It took all Jason's training and restraint not to slam the palm of his hand against the steering wheel. He was pissed off on a level so deep that he had to shut that part of himself down or risk losing focus on what was important—Caroline and her safety.

"Are you okay?" she asked softly.

He nodded, unable to even summon a false smile for her. "I'm good. I'll be better once we're at the hotel, and I'll be perfect once we catch the goddamn bastard who's doing this."

"Did any of the neighbors see anything? I mean, it hasn't been dark for all that long—whoever broke in had to have done it during the day. How does someone burglarize a home in the middle of the day without anyone noticing?"

By blending in.

For a moment, Jason thought he'd said the words aloud. He didn't want to frighten Caroline, because she was already pretty freaked out, but he suspected that whoever had broken into the beach house had been dressed in a way that wouldn't draw attention. A landscaper maybe. Or a cable guy.

He'd send one of his deputies back in the morning to gather information, but for tonight, he just wanted to hold Caroline in his arms and reassure himself that she was safe.

CAROLINE SET HER bag down on the small chair by the bed, and turned to Jason. She could barely see him in the darkness. He secured the locks on the hotel room door before moving over to the windows to pull the shades. Only then did he flip on the small light next to the bed.

Unlike the opulent suite they had stayed in during her first night, this room was a standard room with only the basic amenities. But it was clean and spacious, and the knowledge that she had deputy marshals in the rooms on either side and across the hall made her feel secure. But having Jason in the room with her was what truly made her feel safe.

She watched as he shrugged off his sports jacket and then unfastened his holster, carefully removing the weapon and laying both the gun and the holster on the table near the window, within easy reach. He pulled a second gun out of the back of his waistband and laid that weapon on the table next to the bed. The sight of the guns had a sobering effect on Caroline, but she understood that if she was going to love this man, she had to accept that this was part of his life.

Finally, he turned to her, and she moved into his arms. He held her for a long moment before she leaned slightly back and looked up at him.

"If I haven't said it before, thank you for everything."

A smile touched his mouth. "Everything?"

"You know what I mean," she said, smiling in spite of herself. "I know you didn't have to do this."

"Ah, sweetheart," he said, bracketing her face in his big hands and searching her eyes. "There's no way I couldn't do this. Judge Banks is like a father to me. He's all I have."

"Not anymore," she said, searching his face. "You have me now."

He gave a low groan, and then his mouth was on hers and he was kissing her as if he thought she might vanish at any moment.

"It's okay," she breathed against his mouth. "I'm here."

If she had been terrified about losing him earlier that day, she could sense that he was having similar feelings about her after seeing the house ransacked. But whereas she had already accepted that she was falling in love with Jason, and acknowledged that she wanted him in her life, she didn't think he'd had that same epiphany. She knew instinctively that he wouldn't welcome those feelings. But she also knew that whether he wanted to admit it or not, he was falling for her, too.

Caroline pressed her lips gently against his, shaping the contours of his exquisite mouth. A shudder went through him, and he made a sound. His arms closed tighter around her. Caroline slid her hands along his rib cage and angled her mouth ever so slightly across his, enjoying the sensuality of the kiss.

His arms held her captive as he plundered her mouth, his tongue moving against hers with expert precision. Caroline welcomed his heat and strength, and she could actually feel her body blossom beneath his touch, as if anticipating their joining.

Jason dragged his mouth from hers, trailing his lips over her cheek until her found the juncture of her jaw and throat and pressed his lips to her hammering pulse.

"I want to make love to you," he said, his voice ragged. "I've thought of this all day, but I understand if you don't want to."

She pulled back just enough to stare at him. "Are you kidding?" she asked. "I need for you to make love to me. Right now, what you and I have is the only thing that makes sense in this world. The only thing that's real."

He didn't argue. He simply swept her into his arms before she could utter another word and carried her across the room to the bed. Caroline had never before had a man pick her up so effortlessly, and there was a part of her that thrilled to his masculine strength and the way it made her feel.

Feminine.

Fragile.

He set her on her feet next to the bed and, without giving her a chance to change her mind, cupped her face in his hands and slanted his mouth across hers.

"I could kiss you like this all night," he murmured. "You have the softest lips."

Tilting her head back, he worked his way down her throat, planting light kisses and gentle bites against her flesh, until Caroline shivered with need. His fingers unhurriedly worked the buttons of her shirt; she felt cool air waft against her bare skin. She didn't object when he pushed the shirt from her shoulders, letting the garment drop to the floor until she stood before him in just her bra and pants.

"Let me look at you," he demanded, his voice husky. Caroline blushed as she realized he wasn't just looking at her; he was devouring her with his gaze, and the expression in his eyes made her feel both excited and nervous.

She wanted this. She wanted this beautiful man and the promise of pleasure that lurked in his eyes. She'd never felt this kind of gnawing lust for a man before. Her gaze dropped to his lush mouth, and a sharp stab of desire speared through her. His lips were too tempting.

Keeping her eyes locked with his, Caroline reached behind her and unfastened the clasp of her bra. She didn't miss how Jason swallowed hard in response to that sensuous display. However, instead of immediately relinquishing the undergarment, she held it pressed against her breasts, feeling unaccountably shy. Last night had been amazing, but they'd had the lights off. Now there was no hiding herself from Jason. She felt exposed and oddly vulnerable. The expression in his eyes caused heat to rush through her veins and then pool at her center.

She half expected him to pick her up and toss her onto the bed. Instead, he stroked his hands over her bare skin, his fingers finding the dips and curves of her body with infinite care. He turned his face into the arch of her neck and pressed his mouth against her throat. Then he tugged the bra free from her fingers and let it fall to the floor.

Caroline didn't have time to feel self-conscious before he covered one breast with his big hand, gently massaging her pliant flesh. She gasped at the sensations his touch created, unfamiliar with the cravings of her own body.

His eyes had darkened with desire, the pupils filling up the pale irises. His face was flushed, and the scar on his cheekbone stood out in stark contrast. His nostrils flared, and Caroline knew he was breathing in her scent.

As he cupped her breast, she pushed her hands beneath the hem of his T-shirt. He reflexively tensed, and her fingers skimmed over the muscles that layered his body. She slid her hands higher, reveling in his warm, hard flesh.

He watched her the entire time, and the only indication that her touch affected him was the way his breathing hitched when her fingertips stroked over the small nubs of his nipples.

"Take this off," she whispered, and he complied instantly, reaching behind his head to grab a fistful of shirt and drag it upward.

She couldn't prevent a small indrawn breath. His body was designed for a woman's touch, and she was helpless to prevent herself from running her hand over his chest. She took note of the small scars and imperfections, wondering how he'd gotten the marks.

She traced a long, thin scar that slashed over his ribs, and then a cluster of small, round burn marks just below his collarbone. "Who did this to you?"

He covered her fingers with his own and pressed her

palm flat against his flesh. "It's old history," he muttered. "Forget it."

Caroline understood that these were the injuries he'd sustained as an adolescent, and that he didn't want to talk about it. But she couldn't let it go, any more than she could prevent herself from wanting to soothe the boy he'd once been.

"I can't forget it," she replied. "I need to know what happened to you." She framed his jaw in her hands, feeling the roughness of his whiskers beneath her fingertips. "Trust me."

He stared at her for a long moment, and she could see the wariness in his eyes. Finally, he nodded. "Okay. You should know."

Carefully removing her hands, he walked away, scrubbing a hand across the back of his neck. He radiated tension, and Caroline sensed how difficult it was for him to tell her what she wanted to know. He stood at the window, and when he spoke, his voice was low and rough.

"You know I grew up in Hunters Point. My mother walked out on us when I was about three years old, and I never saw her again." His tone was flat and emotionless, but his entire body was tense. "My father couldn't take care of me on his own, so we moved in with my grandmother." He paused. "Are you sure you want to hear this?"

Caroline nodded. "Yes." What she really wanted was to go to him, and surround him with her love and support, but she understood that he needed to keep some distance between them. "Go on, I'm listening."

"By the time I entered school, my father couldn't hold

a job. He was either too drunk or too high. My grandmother went back to work, which meant she was never around. And all I wanted was to avoid my old man. Because when I didn't—"

"He took his anger at the world out on you," Caroline finished.

Jason snorted. "As long he had enough booze or drugs to make him pass out, things were fine. It was when he couldn't come up with enough cash to buy his next fix that he was dangerous." He angled his head to give her a sardonic look. "When I was eight years old, I started stealing to get money for his heroin. Believe it or not, it was easier than trying to explain the cuts and bruises to my teachers."

Caroline had dealt with literally dozens of child neglect and abuse cases in Richmond, but Jason's story wrenched at her heartstrings. What must it have cost him to deliberately ignore his moral compass, and do something that he knew was wrong?

Dragging the bedsheet around her body, she came to stand just behind him, but restrained herself from touching him. "I'm so sorry."

"I met Eddie when I was twelve. He taught me things that no kid should ever have to learn." He turned to look at her. "Do you know how many homes I broke into as a teenager? How many people I robbed?"

Even in the dim light, Caroline could see the selfloathing on his face, and she ached to reassure him. "You were young, and desperate. And you never physically harmed anyone. You did what you had to, in order to survive."

"I made choices that I knew were wrong, and I didn't care who got hurt."

"That's not true. You did care, or you never would have agreed to my father's conditions. You wanted to change your life, and you did. And the only reason you made those bad choices was to avoid being hurt."

Caroline wound her arms around his waist until they were skin to skin, absorbing the feel of him. "I'll never hurt you," she promised and pressed a kiss directly onto the marks.

With a rough sound of need, Jason lowered his head and caught her mouth in a kiss so passionate that she felt it all the way to her toes. She didn't object when he backed her up to the bed and pushed her gently down across the coverlet, following alongside her.

The bedspread was cool against her bare back, but Jason's skin was hot against her breasts. Breaking the kiss, he worked his way unhurriedly down her throat and over her chest, nuzzling her breasts with his mouth. She watched him, spellbound by the sight of his dark head against her pale skin and feeling the rush of heat and moisture between her legs. When he took a nipple into his mouth and drew deeply on the stiffened tip, she gasped and arched upward, clutching at his shoulders.

He tormented first one breast and then the other, ignoring how she twisted beneath him, her hips shifting restlessly against his. He used his mouth to worship her body, moving from her breasts to her stomach, where he teased her navel with his tongue. His fingers moved to the waistband of her pants and released the fastening in one easy flick of his fingers.

"Yes," she panted as he slowly drew the zipper down. She lifted her torso, helping him to push the garment down over her hips. Jason knelt over her and dragged the pants down the length of her legs until she lay on the bed wearing nothing but her panties.

"Oh, man," he breathed. "You are so damned pretty."

Reaching out, Caroline caught him by the waistband of his jeans and tugged until he came over her on all fours, with her fingers still tucked into his pants.

"Take these off," she urged, needing to see him. "Hurry."

"I'll take them off," Jason said. "But I want to go slow, okay? Last night was amazing, but tonight I want to do things a little differently."

"Okay," she agreed, too eager to see him to tell him that she had no intention of going slow. She was past ready for him. Even now, her panties were soaked with desire for him and her sex throbbed. She had no idea if this was how it was for other women, but she found she enjoyed sex. She was still a little tender from the previous night, but even that evaporated beneath the wave of desire that swept over her now.

Leaning back, Jason unfastened the snap on his jeans, and Caroline helped to push them down over his hips. Her breath caught as she saw his erection tenting the material of his cotton boxer shorts. As he stood up to kick his jeans free, she sat up on the edge of the bed. Reaching out, she laid her hand over the hot ridge of flesh beneath the fabric, thrilling at how he quivered beneath her touch.

"I want to see you," she said and slid her fingers beneath the stretchy waistband to take him in her hand. His breath hissed in through clenched teeth as she curled her fingers around him, and her body pulsed hotly in response.

"You're so gorgeous." She sighed, pushing his boxers down to stroke his length. Glancing upward, she saw Jason watching her through half-closed eyes, his face taut. "You know what I want to do."

"Yeah." His voice came out on a raspy groan.

Caroline smiled. She'd never felt so sexy or powerful before in her life. This guy was the embodiment of masculine strength and beauty, and yet she literally held him trembling in the palm of her hand. The effect was an aphrodisiac.

She cupped his weight from beneath with one hand as she ran her fingers along the velvety shaft with her other hand. The head of his penis was like a ripe plum, and her mouth watered with the need to taste him again, as she'd done last night. Leaning forward, she ran her tongue lightly over the blunt tip.

"Mmm," she murmured. "You taste delicious." Then she took him fully into her mouth.

Jason made a rough sound, a mixture of surprise and arousal. His hands came up to frame her face, his fingers massaging the tender skin behind her ears. Emboldened, Caroline took him deeper, swirling her tongue around him as she used her hand to stroke and caress his length. She pressed her thighs together, squeezing against the sharp throb of desire between them.

"That's enough," he gasped and eased her away, his breath coming fast. "Jesus, where did you learn to do that? I won't last if you keep that up, and I'm not ready for this to be over."

Reluctantly, she released him and let him push her back onto the mattress. Bending over her, he pressed his mouth against her abdomen. The faint stubble on his jaw abraded the tender skin in a way that made her squirm in delicious anticipation.

"You smell great," he said and hooked his thumbs into the elastic waistband of her panties, pulling them down in one smooth movement. His lips drifted over the arch of her ribs and over the swell of her breasts until he reached a nipple and drew it into his mouth. Caroline struggled for breath against the erotic sensations of his tongue and teeth, and she threaded her fingers through his hair, urging him closer.

His warm hand skated over her stomach and lower, urging her legs apart so that he could cup her intimately. Caroline's thighs fell open and she pressed upward against his palm, wanting more of the delicious contact.

"That's it," he rasped against her breast and swirled a finger over her slick flesh, parting her folds and finding the small rise of flesh that thrummed with need. "Oh, man, you're so slippery."

He circled a finger over her clitoris, but it wasn't enough. Caroline's skin went hot and her sex tightened hungrily. Someone moaned and she realized with a sense of shock that it was her. She needed more. Now.

"Soon," Jason promised as if reading her mind. He moved to the floor and knelt between her splayed knees. He stroked a hand along her inner thigh, urging her legs wider, before he bent down and covered her with his mouth.

She gasped and her hips came off the mattress, but he

held her firmly in place as he laved her with his tongue and lips, alternately sucking and licking until she writhed helplessly. When he pressed his tongue against her, tormenting the tiny bud of her clit, she pushed weakly at his shoulders.

"Please," she finally managed in a strangled voice. "Stop. I can't take any more."

Jason laughed softly. He reached down and grabbed his pants from the floor, fishing through the pockets until he produced a small foil packet. He sheathed himself quickly, but Caroline noted that his hands seemed unsteady.

He came over her again, bracing himself with his hands on either side of her. "I'll try to go slow," he said.

"You don't have to go slow," Caroline whispered and slid her hands along his back to cup his lean buttocks and urge him closer. She felt him nudging against her most private spot, and she opened her legs wider, arching upward to meet him.

"I'm sorry," he grunted. "I can't go slowly—"

He thrust forward in one powerful movement, stretching and filling her until he was fully inside her. He didn't move for a long moment, his head bent to hers.

Caroline squeezed experimentally, the walls of her channel tightening around his flesh. Pleasure lashed through her, along with an incredible sense of fullness and a growing need to press herself against him.

Then he began to move, withdrawing slowly and then sinking back into her in a series of bone-melting thrusts. His heated flesh dragged at hers, creating a delicious friction that made her arch upward to meet him. The muscles in his arms flexed as he dipped his head and covered her mouth with his, feasting sensuously on her lips. Caroline heard herself whimper, and she drew her knees back and hooked her feet around his waist, meeting his thrusts eagerly.

She wanted more.

Jason complied, sliding one arm beneath her to press her more intimately against the hard drive of his body. Caroline shivered and wrenched her mouth from his.

"Oh, God," she gasped, clutching at his back. "You feel so good."

"I want you to come." Jason's voice was low and rough.

Caroline could feel the start of an orgasm building where he stroked her, but she didn't want to climax yet.

"Wait," she panted and pushed at his chest.

He raised himself up just enough to look into her face, his own expression taut. "What is it? Am I hurting you?"

"No." She struggled to think coherently. "I'm getting close, and I don't want this to end yet. I want to try something else."

Jason gave a disbelieving laugh, but his movements slowed and then he began to pull back. Caroline gritted her teeth and her body followed his, reluctant to release him. She was so close, and she sensed that he was, too. If they continued, he could take her to heaven in a matter of seconds. But suddenly, she wanted to be the one to take him there—to do things to him that would make him lose control.

She pushed at his shoulders, and, with a bemused smile, he rolled away from her. But Caroline didn't give him a chance to question her; she covered him swiftly with her own body.

"What? Hey—" He laughed uncertainly, but when she dipped her head and traced the whorl of his ear with her tongue, he moaned and collapsed back against the pillows. She pushed his hands up above his head, and slid her own hands down the undersides of his arms, admiring the impressive bulge of his muscles. Her fingers continued downward, and she scooted backward until she straddled his thighs.

Sitting up, she looked down at him. Her breath caught at the sight he made. He was the embodiment of every fantasy she'd ever had. He lay prone beneath her, but there was nothing remotely relaxed about him. His entire body was rigid and his eyes glittered as he watched her through half-closed lids.

"Now it's my turn," she whispered. "I've thought about doing this with you for so long...."

She leaned forward until her breasts brushed against his chest. She traced her lips across his. He cupped the back of her head and drew her down for a more thorough, satisfying kiss. Caroline had intended to tease him, to maintain control of their love play until he begged her to release him. But when he smoothed his free hand along her flank and then reached between them to touch her intimately, she knew she was lost.

She gasped into his mouth and settled more fully against him. He used his hands to splay her thighs even wider where she straddled him. Then there he was, hot and thick, moving into her little bit by little bit, until

Caroline made an incoherent sound and pushed back, thrusting him fully into her.

"Ah," he groaned. "That almost feels too good."

She silently agreed and slowly raised herself up until he was nearly free of her body, before pushing herself down once more, burying him to the hilt. The feeling was unlike anything she had ever experienced before. The hot, throbbing sensation increased as she moved on top of him, gripping him tightly. His hands were on her hips, guiding her, and he watched her face through pleasure-glazed eyes. When he slid his hands upward to cup and knead her breasts, she closed her eyes in mindless bliss.

"Yes," she breathed. "Oh, yes."

"Look at me."

The words were soft but insistent. She opened her eyes and stared down at Jason, seeing the raw, masculine desire on his face.

"I want you to look at me when you come," he rasped. The tautness of his expression told her he was close to losing control, and his words were enough to send her over the brink. Her orgasm slammed into her, and it seemed the only thing anchoring her to earth were Jason's hands, holding her. She might have closed her eyes but for his command.

"Look at me."

And when he reached his own climax, their gazes were locked on one another, until with a last shudder of pleasure, he smiled into her eyes and tugged her down until she lay replete against his chest.

Caroline felt sated and so completely drained that she could barely keep her eyes open. The sound of his heartbeat thudded beneath her ear, lulling her into sleep. With one hand, he stroked lazy patterns over her skin. She was only distantly aware of him pressing a sweet, tender kiss against her face before he tugged the blankets over them both. As she snuggled closer to his warmth, one thought filled her mind—she loved him.

12

CAROLINE WOKE TO the sound of the shower turning on. She lay still for a moment, disoriented, until memories of the previous night came rushing back. Rolling over, she pressed her face into the pillow, breathing in his scent. She'd never known happiness like this even existed. She'd spent years fantasizing about him, but the reality of being with him eclipsed anything she had ever imagined. She'd thought she knew what it was like to be in a physical relationship, but Jason had shattered those notions in less than a day. What she'd never been able to do in previous relationships, he'd coaxed her into doing in less than two days.

A part of her thought she should feel some shame at having given so much so soon, but another part of her wanted to give him even more. She wanted to give him everything and take as much in return.

Glancing at the bedside clock, she saw it was barely five in the morning. They didn't have to be at the hospital for several hours yet, and her imagination swelled with images of Jason standing beneath the steaming spray of water. Feeling bold and a little nervous, Caroline slipped out of bed and retrieved a condom from where Jason kept them in his duffel bag. Then she walked nude to the bathroom, finding the door partially open. She took that as a tacit invitation.

She could just make out his form through the shower enclosure. His body was wreathed in steam. Sucking in a deep breath, she opened the glass door.

He turned, startled. "Caroline."

"Can I come in?"

He stepped back enough to make room for her, his eyes devouring her. Pushing down her own self-consciousness, she stepped into the shower, not missing his growing arousal.

Jason drew her under the water and moved his hand beneath the fall of her wet hair. She lifted her face, feeling the slick slide of his body against hers.

"You do things to me that no other woman has ever done," he muttered, gazing down at her. "You make me crazy."

His lashes were spiky from moisture, and rivulets of water ran down his face and over his neck, tracing wet paths across his chest. Caroline's breath escaped on a sigh. Jason lowered his head and brushed his lips against hers, gently fusing their mouths together. She opened for him, and he pressed forward, guiding her hands to his back to explore the planes and muscles of his shoulders and spine. His body was wet and warm and strong, and she was aware of her body responding to the feel of him against her.

He pulled away, and looked down at her. "Jesus. Look what you've done to me."

Caroline followed his gaze to where his arousal rose against her stomach. She had a sudden, vivid image of him lifting her against the tiled wall and bringing her down onto his straining shaft. Excitement pulsed through her, and she was helpless to prevent herself from curling her fingers around him.

He made a hissing sound of pleasure, and she reached behind him for the small bar of soap. She worked it gently across his impressive chest, watching the streams of water trickle clean paths through the suds. Mesmerized, she smoothed her soapy hands over his body, reveling in the warm, slippery feel of him beneath her palms.

Jason throbbed beneath her touch and eased a hand between her thighs. Her head fell back and she widened her stance to allow him better access.

"Christ. You're so soft," Jason groaned, gently parting her feminine folds. "I could touch you like this forever."

"And I'd let you," she replied with a husky laugh. "Oh, that feels so good."

He supported her around her waist as she leaned back against the tiled wall, but he didn't stop the sensuous rhythm of his hand.

"And to think," she managed between fitful breaths, "that I almost let you shower alone." She gasped as he gently bit the side of her throat.

"What made you change your mind?"

"The thought of you in here. Alone. Naked."

"I don't have any protection."

With a smile, Caroline opened her fisted hand, revealing a small foil packet. She tore it open and quickly covered him. He reached down and grasped her buttocks, lifting her and pressing himself into the cradle of her hips.

"Put your legs around me." His voice was a hoarse growl.

Caroline did. He lifted her higher and braced her against the cool tiled wall. He fused their lips together, and she welcomed the hot slide of his tongue against hers. She gasped as he pressed against the most intimate part of her, before he pushed upward, thrusting himself into her eager body.

She gave a small cry of rapture and raised her legs higher, wrapping them around his hips even as she met the thrusts of his tongue against hers with equal fervor.

God, he felt incredible, all pulsating power. She rode him just as fiercely, gripping his hips tightly with her thighs and using them to lever herself up and down on his shaft. Her fingers speared through his hair, and she moaned into his mouth.

He was everywhere, surrounding her and inside her, his breath mingling with hers and his heart pounding wildly against her own. His skin was slick with water, and his powerful muscles bunched with effort as he pumped into her.

"I can't— I have to—" With a hoarse cry, Jason drove into her one last time, and the raw need in his voice was enough to push Caroline over the edge, as well. She clung to his neck, holding on to him for dear life as she fractured around him in an explosion of pleasure.

They stood locked together like that for several moments before Jason allowed Caroline to slide from his body. Turning the water off, Jason snatched a towel from the rack and wrapped it around her, then used a second towel to cover her hair. He slung a third towel around his lean hips and led her back to the bed.

They lay sprawled across the bedclothes, their breathing still a little uneven. Finally, when she thought she could move again, Caroline raised herself on one elbow and leaned over him, tracing a pattern over his chest with one finger.

"That was unbelievable," she said.

He turned his head and looked at her, and she saw the smile of masculine satisfaction on his face. "Yeah, it was."

Reaching out, he caught a loose tendril of damp hair that had escaped her towel and wound it around his finger. He tugged on it gently, until she was forced to move her face closer to his.

"So who is Patrick?" he asked, releasing her hair and stroking his thumb over her lower lip. "He's called you at least a couple of times."

Caroline wouldn't have thought Jason was capable of jealousy, but the expression in his eyes was so intent that she wondered if she might be wrong.

"He's a social worker in Richmond."

"Go on," he urged.

She couldn't talk about Patrick without revealing the pro bono work she did for Child Protective Services. She didn't know why she was so reluctant to share that with Jason.

"Are you romantically involved?"

"Of course not." She couldn't quite suppress a smile at the thought of kissing Patrick Dougherty. At fifty years old, he carried about thirty extra pounds and his ruddy face bore the evidence of a hard life. He drank too much, but she couldn't even blame him for that. He was a good man, and he'd seen some terrible things during his years as a social worker. She'd probably drink, too, if she was in his position.

"Then why are you smiling?"

Caroline gave Jason an exasperated look. "He and I have worked together on some child welfare cases, okay? But he's old enough to be my father, and even if I was into older guys, he's not my type."

He looked at her with sharp interest. "You work child welfare? I thought you handled corporate law."

"I do some pro bono work on the side for the city of Richmond."

"What kind of pro bono work?"

Caroline hesitated. He had shared his background with her. The very least she could do was tell him about her work, even if it meant he would guess the impact he had made on her life. "I'm a child advocate, mostly working with kids who've run away from home or gotten into trouble. I try to keep them out of juvie, make sure they have a safe place to go every night."

Jason was silent for several minutes. "You're more like your father than you want to admit. Does your pro bono work have anything to do with a certain angry kid that your dad once rescued?"

She risked a glance at his face, but his expression was so tender that she found herself coming clean. "You're the reason for everything I do, every decision I make. I couldn't even come back to San Francisco because I was too afraid I would see you, and that you'd reject me like you did all those years ago."

"You know why I had to do that."

Caroline nodded. "Do you think my father ever guessed?"

"What? That I had the hots for his daughter?"

"Oh, right," she scoffed. "No, that I had the hots for you."

Jason gave a half smile. "I think he knew. I wanted to know everything that was going on in your life, and I wasn't always so subtle or smooth in getting the information from him that I wanted."

Caroline stared at him. "You used to ask my father about me?"

He actually had the grace to look embarrassed. "Well, not directly, of course. But I pretty much knew everything you were doing, even when I was away at school."

"I never knew. My father never said a word."

"He probably didn't want to encourage it. I'm sure I wasn't exactly what he'd envisioned for his daughter."

"That's not true. You were the son he always wanted." Dipping her head, she pressed a lingering kiss against his mouth. "For myself, you were just the guy I always wanted."

She was unprepared when Jason hauled her into his arms and hugged her tightly against his chest, his face buried in her neck.

"I'm glad."

JASON DIDN'T WANT to leave Caroline alone, but he was anxious for any news about the break-in at the beach house and if the subsequent inspection of the property had yielded any clues. But there was no way he was letting her out of his sight, even to make some phone calls.

There was a new intimacy between them, and he was aware that her eyes followed him when she thought he wasn't looking. For his part, he just wanted to keep her locked in the hotel room until an arrest was made, and maybe even afterward. He wasn't taking any chances with her safety.

After their shower, they dressed and Jason ordered breakfast from room service. She had been adamant that he review the files on the medical malpractice cases and that he have the FBI look into the families involved. As a U.S. marshal, Jason had certainly seen people do violent things in the name of love, but his gut instinct told him that the shooter was either connected to Eddie Green or Conrad Kelly. Both men were formidable in their respective spheres. They had connections and could easily have ordered the attack without fear of reprisal. But he agreed that they would follow up on the malpractice cases.

"So what do we do now?" she asked. She sat on the bed, the pillows propped behind her as she reviewed yet another case file. She'd retrieved a narrow pair of reading glasses from her overnight bag, and they sat perched on the end of her nose as she simultaneously ate a fruit parfait and read through the documents. With her hair down and wearing a loose pair of pajama bottoms and a camisole, she looked incredibly sexy.

"Since when do you wear glasses?" Jason asked, sipping a mug of strong coffee as he scrolled through the messages on his smart phone.

"Since forever," she replied absently. "See...there's something you don't know about me. I even wore glasses back when I was in high school, or at least I was supposed to." She flashed him a mischievous smile. "I didn't think they were sexy, so I refused to wear them."

There was a knock at the door, and Deputy Black called Jason's name through the door. Slanting a look at Caroline, he opened the door and let the deputy in.

"They made an arrest last night," Colton said. "Two men have confessed."

Caroline threw the files to one side and climbed to her feet, yanking her reading glasses off. "Are you sure? Who was it?"

Colton looked at Jason as if for permission. Jason nodded curtly.

"After the break-in at the Santa Cruz house, the police received an anonymous tip that two men were seen in the vicinity of the Sea Cliff residence on the night of the shooting."

"Go on," Jason said.

"Who called it in?" Caroline interrupted. "Are they sure they have the right men?"

Colton looked at her, his expression serious. "My understanding is that the police just brought them in about ten minutes ago, and they're still being questioned. But one of the men did admit to the shooting."

Caroline turned to Jason. "We have to get down there. I want to see these guys for myself."

"Do they have names?" Jason asked.

Deputy Black nodded. "Yeah. They're two of San-chez's men."

Jason's eyes narrowed. "Really?"

"He's the Mexican drug lord who wanted to serve the remainder of his sentence in Mexico?" Caroline looked at Jason for confirmation.

He nodded absently. "Yes, but it doesn't make sense. Why would his men confess?"

"My understanding is that whoever called in the tip was able to provide a tag number for the car they were driving. The police went to the address and found the men. Someone had worked them over pretty good. From what I hear, they practically begged the police to take them in."

Caroline frowned. "But they did confess."

"That's correct."

"So then it's over?" Caroline turned to look at Jason again.

He didn't want to crush her hopes, but the news just didn't make sense to him. If the men had been beaten, it was because they had botched the job, or someone with even more influence than Sanchez had intimidated the men into confessing.

"Deputy, I'm sending you over to the police department to oversee the questioning. I'll bring Caroline over to the hospital. Until we have solid proof that these are our guys, we're not doing anything differently."

"But, Jason—"

"I'm not taking any chances," he said, forestalling whatever argument she might have presented. "I don't know who these guys are or if they really are part of Sanchez's gang or why they would confess to the shooting. They must know that if they implicate Sanchez, he'll have them killed. Being in prison won't keep them safe."

Caroline sighed heavily and walked over to the far side of the room, hugging her arms around her middle. Jason's eyes lingered on her for several seconds, and then he turned his attention back to Colton.

"Get over to the station and check it out," he said. "If anything seems out of place with their story, let me know."

Colton nodded and looked over at Caroline. "What will you do?" he asked quietly.

Jason followed his gaze. "Deputy Mitchell and I will bring her over to the hospital to see her father, and we'll wait for your call."

When they were alone again, she pivoted toward him. "Do you think it was them? Sanchez's men? I mean, it's possible, right? Sanchez is on your list of potential suspects, based on how my father ruled against him."

"It's possible that Sanchez's men are culpable," he conceded. "But I'll have the FBI look into those malpractice cases, just as a precaution. Until we know for certain these men were responsible, you're still under my protection. That's not going to change."

13

CAROLINE SAT BY her father's bedside, holding his hand in her own. The doctors, satisfied with his progress, had removed the ventilator, and he was breathing on his own. He still had a number of tubes coming out of him, but he did seem to be resting more comfortably.

She desperately wanted him to regain consciousness, however briefly, but he hadn't opened his eyes again. The doctors had assured her that this was normal, and that he was, in fact, going to make a full recovery.

Caroline just had to be patient. But she'd been by his bedside for nearly six hours, and there'd been no visible change in his condition. She looked up as the door opened and Jason came in. He stepped over to the window and exchanged quiet words with Deputy Mitchell. The deputy glanced over at her and left the room.

Caroline rose to her feet. "What is it?"

"The men recanted."

She put out a hand and grasped her father's bed rail for balance. "What do you mean?"

Jason's eyes were so sympathetic that she knew he didn't want to tell her what he'd learned. "Miguel Gonzales and Roberto Calvo are two of Sanchez's top men, and, yes, they initially confessed to shooting the judge." He scrubbed a hand over his hair. "But after questioning, they retracted their story."

She shrugged, giving him a bewildered look. "So what? They probably think they can get away with it. I'd recant, too, if I thought it would gain me my freedom."

"No, it's not like that," he said. "Believe me, I wish it was that easy. These men were coerced into a confession."

"How?"

"They were beaten and their families were threatened. They believed they had no choice but to confess or they would be killed."

Caroline stared at him in astonishment. "But who would do that? Who would have that kind of power?"

"Eddie Green."

"And you think he had those men beaten?"

"I do."

"But why? It makes no sense."

"He and the Sanchez gang have been in competition for years. Eddie used to control the entire Hunters Point region, until the Sanchez gang moved in about six years ago. There's been a territory dispute going on since then. Eddie considers Hunters Point his terrain, but the Sanchez gang has gained a strong foothold."

"So Eddie thought he could intimidate these men into confessing, and force them out of Hunters Point?"

"Something like that. With Sanchez behind bars,

Eddie probably thought he could further weaken their faction by getting rid of the top leaders." Jason blew out a hard breath. "But there's nothing to indicate these men were anywhere near Sea Cliff the night of the shooting."

"If Eddie wants them gone, why beat them? Why didn't he just kill them?"

"He knew they wouldn't be convicted. He was sending a message to Sanchez that his men are weak, and that at any time, Eddie can get to them."

"So this had nothing to do with my father and everything to do with a gang war?" Caroline couldn't keep the dismay out of her voice.

"I'm sorry. I wish I had better news for you. Eddie Green saw this as an opportunity to send a message, but you're right—it has nothing to do with your father's shooting. Eddie was the one who called in the tip on the license plates and led the police to Sanchez's men." Jason pulled her into his arms, pressing her face into his shoulder and soothing his hands over her back. "It was all just a game to him."

"I just want this to be over." Her words were muffled against his body. "I want it to end."

"Caroline." The voice was weak and raspy.

She lifted her head and slowly looked toward the bed where her father lay. "Daddy?"

William's eyes were slightly open, and he was looking directly at her. With a cry, she pulled free from Jason's arms and hurried to his bedside, bending over him and grasping his frail hand in both of hers.

"I'm here, Daddy. I'm here," she said, aware that her face was wet with tears.

"Caroline."

"It's okay." She smoothed her hand over his brow. "I'm here, and everything is going to be fine."

She looked over her shoulder to where Jason stood at her side. His expression softened as he looked at her father, and he put a hand on her shoulder, squeezing gently.

"Do you remember what happened, sir?" Jason asked.

William Banks's face wrinkled in concentration, and then he gave an almost imperceptible shake of his head.

"Don't worry," Caroline reassured him. "I just want you to rest now." She glanced at Jason. "Please, go get the doctor."

He crossed the room and opened the door, speaking quickly to the guards who stood outside before closing the door and coming back to the bedside.

"Someone will be right in," he said, but his eyes were on Judge Banks.

"Always knew you should be together," the older man said in a thin, gravelly voice.

"Daddy," Caroline protested, embarrassed. "We don't need to talk about this right now."

The door opened, and a doctor and two nurses entered, rolling a tray of equipment with them. The doctor looked at Caroline and gave her a quick smile.

"I told you he'd progress quickly," he said to her. "You're welcome to stay in the room while we examine him."

Caroline looked at her father, but he had closed his eyes again. "No," she demurred. "We'll let you do your job. We'll be right back, Dad."

Jason and Caroline stepped out into the corridor,

where Deputy Mitchell and the other guards stood. She sagged against Jason, feeling a little weak from the force of her relief.

"He's going to be okay," she said, looking at him. "He's really going to be okay."

Jason supported her, letting her lean against him, with a strong arm around her shoulders. "I hope you're right."

In that moment, Caroline knew she wouldn't be returning to Virginia. She'd call Arthur MacInness, and let him know that she was leaving the law firm. He'd understand. Then she'd let Patrick Dougherty know that she wouldn't be coming back. She only hoped that the lawyer who had taken over her cases was working out. She knew from firsthand experience how difficult it was not to get involved with the kids once you'd heard their stories.

But her life was here now, in California. Her father needed her. And she needed Jason.

"I'm staying here," she murmured.

He nodded. "Absolutely. I'll have one of the men grab us something to eat from the cafeteria."

"No," she said, looking up at him. "I'm staying here, in California. I'm not returning to the East Coast."

For a moment he just stared at her, uncomprehending. Then his whole expression changed. "Caroline, your father won't be in the hospital forever. Eventually, he'll be well enough to return home, maybe even go back to his job."

"I know. Even if he does decide to go back to work, I'm not returning to Richmond."

"What changed your mind?"

"I have too much for me here," she said softly. "Everything I care about is here in California."

He tilted his head, waiting. "Not just in San Francisco?"

"In San Francisco, and in San Diego."

He bent toward her and lowered his voice. "If we weren't being watched by every man in this hallway, I'd kiss you right now."

Without looking at the other men, Caroline raised herself on tiptoe and planted a kiss directly on his mouth.

"Consider that a down payment," she said, smiling into his eyes. "That's the first thing I'm looking forward to, once this whole thing is over."

"What is?"

"The right to kiss you whenever I want, without anyone passing judgment."

The door to her father's room opened, and the doctor stepped out. "He's in a considerable amount of pain, so I've increased his morphine," he said. "But I'm really pleased with his progress, and we'll be moving him out of ICU within the next day or so." He looked at Jason. "He has no memory of what happened to him. He said the last thing he remembers is going to bed the night before. That's pretty common with a traumatic event."

"Will he regain those memories?" Jason asked.

The doctor shrugged. "It's hard to say. He might, but I've seen cases where the patient never recalls the incident."

"You're not making my job any easier, doc," Jason said.

The doctor gave him a sympathetic smile and slapped

him lightly on the back. "The judge says you always get your man, so I have no doubt you'll catch who did this to him."

"Can I see him?" Caroline asked.

"Of course, but we just sedated him." He gave Jason a sympathetic look. "You'll have to save your questioning for later, Marshal."

Jason nodded.

In his room, Caroline stood by her father's bed and watched him sleep. "I remember when my mother died, and I refused to leave my bedroom for six days," she said thickly. "I was just a toddler. I wouldn't even go to her funeral. I thought maybe if I didn't leave my room, I could still believe she was somewhere in the house."

Jason stroked her back. "The judge said you had a pretty tough time after she died."

"He left me just long enough to go to her service, but otherwise he never left my side. Even after the funeral, when we had a house filled with people, he stayed in my room with me. He never lost his patience with me or tried to force me to come downstairs or tell me that I had to face the truth." She turned and looked at Jason. "He was just there, ready to give me whatever it was that I needed."

"He loves you very much."

"I want to be here for him," she said. "Until he's ready to leave this hospital, I want to be sure he has everything he needs."

"All he needs is you, Caroline."

She nodded, blinking back tears. "I know, but would you mind if we go over to the Sea Cliff house? I'd like to pick up some of his personal things and bring them back here. He'd be happier, I think."

"Sure. The investigators are finished at the house, so I see no reason why we can't do that."

JASON HAD BEEN RIGHT—the crime tape was gone. Pulling into the driveway of the home, nobody would ever guess that the house had been the scene of a horrific crime just days earlier.

"I sent a cleaning crew out here yesterday," he told her, shutting off the engine. "You won't see anything in the front entrance to upset you."

Caroline nodded. "Thanks."

Jason glanced in his rearview mirror; Deputies Black and Mitchell had pulled in behind them. "Let's give them a few minutes to secure the house, and then we can go in."

They sat in the car while the two men did a quick sweep of the property and the house before coming out to the porch to wave them in.

"All clear," Jason said.

Caroline hadn't been inside the house in years, and entering the large kitchen, she was immediately struck by how little it had changed in her absence. She realized it was one of the things she loved about being home— she could always count on it feeling familiar and safe.

"There's nobody else in the house," Jason said, coming to stand beside her. "The staff won't return until your father is discharged and sent home. Unless, of course, you want them here sooner."

Caroline shook her head. "No, that's not necessary.

I'll see that their wages are paid for the time they're not working, but there's no point in them coming to the house. They may not even want to. Until the shooter is caught, I don't think I'd want to come back here."

"You're safe," Jason assured her.

Caroline knew without being told that the two deputies had taken up positions near the front and back doors of the house, and that nobody would get past them.

"I'm going to run upstairs and pack a small bag," she said.

"I'll come with you."

She paused. "You don't have to, Jason. You said I'm safe."

"Call me old-fashioned," he murmured. "I take my job seriously."

She was acutely aware of him following her up the wide, curving staircase to the second floor. She was filled with bittersweet memories of the times when Jason had stayed in their house during his college years, but had never seemed to notice she existed. She'd been so head over heels crazy for him.

She still was.

"Have you ever been upstairs?" she asked now.

"Sure."

She glanced at him. "I think there was a reason my father put your room down on the first floor."

He grinned up at her. "Absolutely. Although, until you were about fifteen, you were just this cute little annoyance."

Caroline laughed, recalling how she used to spy on

Jason, thinking he wouldn't notice. "And after I was fifteen?"

He expression was rueful. "I'm ashamed to admit that I did check you out. But I never would have crossed that line with you. It was just hard to ignore you when you seemed determined to wear as little clothing as possible."

They'd reached the second floor, and Caroline paused on the landing. "I was determined to make you notice me."

"Oh, I noticed," he said, laughing. "And the older you got, the more I couldn't help noticing."

"You seemed so different from any of the boys I went to high school with."

"Yeah, I was a lot older."

She studied him now. "No, it had more to do with your attitude. You seemed a little dangerous, and I always wondered, after you left, if I'd ever see you again. You were a little bit like a wild creature, always on the verge of bolting for freedom."

"I felt a little wild back then."

She turned and continued down the carpeted hallway until she reached the door to her bedroom. After opening it, she stood back so that he could see. "This is where I did all my fantasizing about you."

The room was spacious and airy, with sweeping views of the water. The canopy bed was draped with sheer curtains, and the walls were covered in posters, while decorative minilights dangled from the ceiling. Floor-to-ceiling bookshelves contained her youthful collection of novels, music boxes and stuffed animals, and Caroline knew that if she were to open the wide closet doors, all her old clothing and shoes would still be neatly lined up.

"You never thought to redecorate?" Jason asked wryly. "I don't think this room has changed since you were fifteen."

She smiled. "Nope. I told my dad that he could convert it to another guest bedroom, but he said he liked it just the way it was." She paused. "He said it reassured him that there was still innocence and goodness in the world."

"I understand what he meant."

"Do you ever want to do something different?" she ventured.

"Nope."

"But you could be a trial lawyer with your background," she said.

"Can you honestly see me striding through a courtroom, making impassioned speeches?" he asked. "I spent ten years in law enforcement before I was appointed to the marshal position. This is where I belong."

Caroline nodded. She knew exactly what he meant. She recalled that moment when she realized she was meant to work with underprivileged children. She'd had a sense of complete fulfillment. While corporate law might be more lucrative, she would never find it more satisfying.

"What about you?" Jason asked. "Ever see yourself as a trial lawyer?"

She gave a surprised laugh. "Me? No. I've thought about using my trust fund to set up a foundation for needy kids." She sensed his sharp interest. "I really enjoyed the pro bono work I did in Richmond for the child welfare office. I felt like I was making a difference."

"That's a noble endeavor," he finally replied. "What about working as a child advocate here in San Francisco?" He gave her a wry grin. "Trust me, if I'd had someone like you on my side back when I was a kid, things might have been very different."

Caroline sobered. "But then I might never have met you. You wouldn't have ended up in my father's courtroom, and you certainly wouldn't have spent time with us while you finished college."

"And you wouldn't have spent half your time watching me when you thought I wasn't looking," he said, his tone teasing.

Her eyes widened. "You knew I used to spy on you?"

Grinning, he pulled her into his arms. "Like I said, I knew everything about you."

They stared at each other for several long seconds. Jason swallowed, and his gaze dropped to her mouth.

She placed her hands lightly against his chest and pressed her lips sweetly to his. The moment their lips met, heat flared. With a rough groan, Jason captured her face between his big hands and slanted his mouth across her own. She didn't resist when she felt the intrusion of his tongue against hers, and then there was only a slow burn that made her nipples ache and her center throb.

She wound her arms around his neck, speared her fingers through his hair and reveled in the hard, solid feel of him, flush against her from chest to knees. He slid a hand to the base of her spine and pressed her forward so that she could feel his growing erection beneath his jeans.

In another second, she was going to drag him into her childhood bedroom, throw him across the pristine white bedspread and do all the things that she'd ever fantasized about doing to him.

The sound of a car door slamming nearby startled them both, and they broke apart, their breathing a little labored. Stepping past her, Jason moved swiftly into her bedroom and over to the side window. She followed him, and they both looked outside.

A car had pulled into the driveway of the house next door, and a woman had climbed out of the passenger seat. She wore a plain beige uniform with a white collar and cuffs and white service shoes. As they watched, the car reversed slowly and backed into the street before driving away.

"That's the neighbor's housekeeper," Jason noted.

She remembered the woman from that first day, when she had insisted on seeing the spot where her father had been shot. Now the woman carried two large shopping sacks in her arms, and Caroline could see a long loaf of crusty bread and a leafy vegetable poking out of the top.

"She must be the cook," she murmured. "Or maybe she does both. Looks like she has something good planned for dinner."

They watched as the woman climbed the steps to the back door and then pulled out her house key, struggling to balance the two sacks of groceries and her pocketbook. She glanced once over at their house and gave a quick nod of acknowledgment. Caroline knew that one of the deputies stood guard on the back porch, so she must have just become aware of him observing her.

"Poor thing," Caroline said. "She must be completely freaked out."

Unable to juggle the groceries and her pocketbook, she set her purse down by her feet and quickly unlocked the door. She disappeared inside, and then returned a scant second later to scoop up the pocketbook and close the door firmly behind her.

"Yeah," Jason said thoughtfully. "She didn't look too happy."

14

THE FOLLOWING DAY, Caroline stood near her father's bed and carefully arranged the dozens of flowers, potted plants, balloons and cards that had arrived daily since the shooting. He'd been moved out of the intensive care unit and into a private room and could finally accept personal items.

While the judge spent most of his time sleeping, he'd been awake for intermittently longer periods of time. Not wanting to tire him out, Caroline had sat quietly reading.

Jason was never more than a few steps away, although she noted that his guard seemed to be lowering a bit, now that her father had regained consciousness. He seemed convinced that the judge would eventually recall exactly who had come to his door that fateful night, and that an arrest was imminent.

Now he stood by the windows, conversing in low tones with Deputy Black and two FBI agents. Caroline glanced at her father, but he was sound asleep, his mouth slack.

The last thing she wanted was for him to overhear any of the conversation and become distressed.

Seeing him so relaxed, she turned her ear to Jason's discussion. She knew the FBI had recovered fingerprints from the beach house in Santa Cruz but had not been able to come up with a match. They'd also pulled a second partial footprint from the soil beside the house that seemed to match the one they'd retrieved from the Sea Cliff house.

There was no longer any doubt that whoever had attacked her father had also ransacked the beach house.

"This involved more than one person," Jason said. "Unless they brought a ladder, which there's no evidence they did, one person couldn't have reached the electrical service drop without help.

The FBI agents seemed in agreement with his assessment, and they had stepped up security at both the houses and the hospital. They had set up a command post of sorts outside her father's room, with several laptops and communications systems that allowed them to speak to their teams located outside the hospital.

"The neighbors can't recall seeing or hearing anything unusual at the house in Santa Cruz," the first agent said. "They said there was a downpour that evening that drove everyone indoors for about two hours. My guess is that's when the perps entered the house. They may have even parked their car outside the area, so as not to arouse suspicion."

"What about the footprint?" Jason asked. "Are you sure it's a match to the one found at the primary residence?"

"Absolutely," the second agent said. "The rain actually worked in our favor, since it softened the soil. Again, it's only a partial print, as if the perp was walking on his or her toes."

"Her?" Jason's voice sharpened.

"It's only a theory," the first agent said. "We don't have the complete footprint, so there's no way of telling the exact size of the shoe, but it looks to be on the small side. So it could be a male with smaller feet or it could be a female."

Caroline watched as Jason's face grew thoughtful; then he excused himself and walked over to where she sat. She stood up and drew him over toward the door, out of earshot.

"I heard," she said. "Why would any woman do this?"

Jason shook his head. "I don't know. Did your father ever mention a female friend? Someone he was seeing, either romantically or maybe as a friend?"

"No," she said fervently, keeping her voice low. "To my knowledge, my father lived like a monk after he lost my mother. He never once brought a woman back to the house, and if he ever had a date, I didn't know about it."

Jason smiled grimly. "No doubt part of his plan to keep you innocent."

She gaped at him. "Are you telling me that my father did have relationships?"

He gave her a helpless look. "He's a man, Caroline. He's also wealthy and powerful. I'm sure there are a lot of women who find him very attractive. Just because he didn't bring them home, or tell you about them, doesn't mean they didn't exist."

She felt a little stunned. "But I wanted him to date," she said. "I used to try to play matchmaker for him, and he'd just laugh and tell me that he was a hopeless cause. He said I was the only girl for him. Eventually, I just gave up, because he seemed so dead set against it."

"He was only dead set against bringing another woman into your life," Jason said softly. "He loved your mother very much, and I don't think he ever wanted to replace those memories. He wanted you to remember her, too."

Caroline felt tears prick the back of her eyelids. "But I don't really remember her. I have only vague, hazy memories of her." She smiled at him. "But they're all happy memories. Sometimes a song or a particular scent will bring her face into clear focus, but if I try and picture what she looked like, I can't."

"Hey, it's okay," Jason said, pulling her into his arms. "I lost my mother when I was very young, too. At least you have those good memories. I couldn't even tell you what color hair my mother had."

She pulled back to look at his face. Although she knew his homelife had been difficult, she didn't know the details, and her father had refused to discuss them with her.

"What happened to her?" she asked.

Jason shrugged. "I don't know. She left us when I was just a toddler. My father refused to talk about her, and my grandmother would only say she was trash."

Her heart constricted. "Oh, Jason, I'm sure that isn't true. Have you ever tried to locate her?"

He nodded. "A couple of times, but I never came up with any leads on her."

She hugged him hard. "I'm sure she had her reasons for leaving and not bringing you with her."

"That's what the counselors told me," he said. At her questioning look, he sighed. "After I ended up in court, and your father decided I was worth saving, he pulled me out of Hunters Point and sent me to a residential school for troubled youths. Part of the program to rehabilitate me involved meeting with counselors every day." He gave a huff of laughter. "I was a pretty angry kid, ergo I had a lot of counseling."

"My father did that?" she asked. Her father had given many kids a second chance, but she hadn't understood the extent of his generosity. "He sent you to a private school?"

"He did. Your father is the only reason I didn't end up like Eddie Green, because back then I was doing my best to imitate him."

"I had no idea," Caroline admitted. "I mean, I knew that he sometimes took a special interest in juvenile offenders, and did what he could to give them a second chance, but I had no idea he did so much."

"I'm not saying he did that for every kid," he said. "But what he did for me changed my life."

"What he did for you changed my life, too," she said tenderly, gazing up at him. "I would never have met you otherwise."

Jason chuckled. "I'm not sure if your father could have looked into the future and seen us together that he would have been so eager to help me."

She gave him a tolerant look. "That's not true. He loves you like a son. You heard him earlier—he always thought we should be together. He just about gave us his blessing."

This time, there was no doubting Jason's amusement. "He's strung out on morphine, sweetheart. He had no idea what he was saying."

Before she could respond, his cell phone began to beep. He glanced at the screen and then over at the two agents. "This is my office. Sorry, but I need to take this call."

The two agents retreated to the corridor, and Jason moved to the far side of the room to speak quietly into the phone. Caroline went back to her father's bed, surprised when she saw he was awake.

"Hey, Dad," she said, leaning over him. "How are you feeling?"

"Tired," he said weakly, giving her a wan smile.

"Go back to sleep," she urged him. "Everything is okay, and the doctors say you're going to be up and around in no time at all. I'd rest while you can."

"Thirsty."

Because of his injury, he'd not yet been cleared for solid foods and still got most of his nutrients intravenously. Caroline knew she couldn't give him any water, but she could let him suck on some ice chips. Reaching for the cup where she kept his ice, she saw it had melted to several inches of water, which was tepid, at best.

"I'm just going to refill your ice bucket," she said. "I'll be right back."

Scooping up his empty pitcher and his ice bucket, she got Jason's attention, and held up both items so that he would know where she was going. He covered the phone with his hand.

"Ask Deputy Black to go with you," he said. "He's right outside."

She nodded and slipped out of the room. In the corridor, she saw Deputy Black in conversation with the two FBI agents at the far end of the hall. A new guard, whom Caroline didn't recognize, sat outside the door.

"I'm just going to refill my father's ice bucket," she said to the guard.

He shrugged, as if it was no consequence to him what she did. Glancing at Deputy Black, she hesitated. The guard clearly didn't care if she stepped down the hallway to where the ice machine stood, and with so many law enforcement personnel in the hallway, Caroline couldn't imagine a safer place for her to be. Unwilling to disturb the deputy for such a small errand, she walked in the opposite direction, away from the room.

She wasn't as familiar with the layout of this floor as she had been with the ICU, and when she reached the end of the corridor without seeing the ice machine, she paused for a moment to get her bearings.

"The ice machine is to your right, honey," said a passing nurse. She indicated the adjacent corridor. "Halfway down, on your left, next to the ladies' room."

"Thank you."

Caroline walked swiftly in the direction that the nurse had indicated. Halfway down the hallway, she located the machine and paused to fill the bucket. While she waited for the ice to dispense, a movement caught her eye, and she looked to her right to see a man carrying a large bouquet of flowers. He had paused almost directly beside her to study a hospital directory that hung on the wall.

Caroline watched him covertly. She guessed him to be in his thirties, and he was distinctly Latino. He was dressed in baggy jeans and heavy work boots, and he wore a bulky jacket over his large frame, despite the warm temperature outside. A baseball cap was pulled low over his eyes. As if sensing her scrutiny, he turned and looked directly at her.

Caroline panicked.

Jerking upright, she glanced swiftly back the way she had come. The corridor seemed ominously long and empty. The door to the ladies' room was right next to her, and without thinking she pushed her way inside. With her heart hammering, she stood inside the door and waited, the ice bucket raised in one hand, but nobody followed her. After a moment, she lowered the bucket, aware that her heart was still slamming against her ribs.

Once she realized she wasn't in danger, the adrenaline rush ended, leaving her weak and shaking. She dragged in a deep breath, forcing herself to calm down. Disgusted by her own fearfulness, she walked over to the bank of sinks and set the bucket down. She braced her hands on the counter, willing her heart to slow its frantic pace.

After a moment, she gave a feeble laugh. She was in a hospital, for Pete's sake, with half a dozen police, FBI agents and deputy marshals within shouting distance. No one was going to hurt her, and even if they tried, one scream from her would bring them all running.

Now that her panic had subsided, Caroline realized she really did need to use the bathroom, and she stepped into one of the stalls. She had no sooner sat down then she heard the bathroom door open and footsteps entering. For one wild, petrifying instant, she thought it was the man with the flowers, and that he'd come in to kill her. She was halfway to her feet, when the person entered the stall beside her own. Beneath the divider, Caroline could see a woman's feet, encased in a pair of white service shoes. She relaxed.

Not a man. Not a killer.

A nurse.

The nurse lowered a pocketbook to the floor of the stall, and Caroline raised her eyebrows. Didn't the woman know there was a hook on the back of the door? There was no way she'd ever let her own pocketbook come in contact with a bathroom floor, no matter how clean and hygienic it appeared. Her eyes narrowed briefly on the handbag, thinking it seemed vaguely familiar, before she brushed the thought away.

She left the stall a moment later and moved to the sink to wash her hands. Bending over, she splashed cool water against her face. She heard the flush, and then the stall door opened. Caroline straightened, reaching for the paper towels, when her eyes met those of the other woman.

With a swift gasp, she spun around. Not a nurse, but the housekeeper from next door to where her father lived. What had the police officer said her name was? Marisola Perez?

"What are you doing here?" she managed, but she thought she already knew.

Marisola's features were twisted in grief and hatred,

and tears filled her dark eyes. Holding her purse in one hand, she reached into the bag and withdrew a gun. Letting the handbag drop to the floor, she advanced on Caroline, who was too stunned to move, never mind scream.

"An eye for an eye," she said brokenly. "A child for a child. I lost my daughter, and your father did nothing. My daughter came to this very hospital for an appendix operation. A simple procedure, the doctors said. But she died." A sob escaped her, and she pressed her free hand to her mouth. "She came out of the surgery with such severe brain damage that she never woke up again. I had to pull the plug that kept her alive. No mother should ever have to do that!"

Her voice had risen, and Caroline could see the woman was shaking. Caroline gripped the edge of the sink, her eyes on the gun. "I know your story," she said softly. "I'm so sorry for what happened to you. For what you went through."

"I have had to live without my daughter," Marisola cried. "I wanted justice, but your father denied me that. I'm glad now that he didn't die when I shot him. I've had to suffer life without my child. Now he will know that same pain!"

With a hoarse cry, she raised the gun. Without conscious thought, Caroline grabbed the ice bucket and flung it at the woman. Ice and water flew everywhere, and Marisola flinched as ice cubes struck her in the face. There was a sharp retort as the gun discharged, and Caroline felt the air stir near her face before the mirror exploded behind her.

Marisola's feet slipped on the wet surface of the floor,

and her face registered her surprise as she lost her balance. Her arms pinwheeled as she sought to regain her footing. Caroline spun away as Marisola tried to aim the gun at her.

Then the door of the bathroom exploded inward, and Jason was there, his own weapon drawn, followed hard by Colton and the FBI agents. In an instant, Caroline was in his arms, and the three other men restrained the woman, knocking the gun from her hand as they bore her down to the floor and wrenched her arms behind her back.

Marisola was sobbing and screaming at the same time, deep, anguished sobs that were full of grief and fury. "My daughter is dead, and he didn't care," she cried. "It's only right that he lose his daughter, that he knows how it feels!"

The two FBI agents hauled the struggling woman to her feet and dragged her, still screaming, out of the bathroom. Caroline clung to Jason, unwilling to let him go.

"Are you hurt?" he asked, setting her away from him and sweeping her body with one all-encompassing look. "Did she hurt you?"

"No, I'm okay."

"Christ," he muttered. "Thank God."

He hauled her back into his arms, and she could feel the deep thump of his heart beneath her ear. His breathing was a little uneven, and when he finally pulled back to tip her face up, she realized his hand was trembling.

"I'm okay," she repeated, humbled and chastened by his obvious fear for her safety.

His eyes blazed down at her, and now that she was

safe, she saw the anger that had crept in. His fingers tightened around her upper arms where he held her.

"I want to throttle you, Caroline Banks. What in hell were you thinking? You know better than to go anywhere alone. We've been through this over and over. Jesus!"

He released her to jerk away, raking a hand over his hair. When he turned back around, he was clearly still furious but had managed to regain some control over his temper. He held his arm out to her. "C'mon, let's go."

She moved toward him, and he held her snugly against his side as he led her out of the bathroom. In the corridor, a crowd had gathered, drawn by the gunshot and Marisola's impassioned screams. Caroline could see her being led away by two police officers. Next to the ice machine, the man with the flowers stood with his back pressed against the wall, his eyes wide with shock as he watched the scene. Jason led her away, walking with her until they reached a quiet spot with nobody else in sight. Only then did he push her up against the wall, pinning her there with the hard weight of his body. He bracketed her face in his hands, searching her eyes.

"I don't ever want to go through something like that again," he muttered. "When I think how close I came to losing you—"

"No," Caroline said, covering his hands with her own. "You didn't. I'm fine. She wouldn't have hurt me. I'm strong, and I would have stopped her."

He gave a huff of disbelieving laughter. "Caroline, she had a gun. She would have killed you."

"But she didn't."

"And she won't get another chance," Jason vowed.

"Officers are on their way to her residence right now to gather information. You're not leaving my sight until we figure out if she acted alone, or if she had an accomplice."

"My guess is that she acted alone," Caroline said. "She was a grief-stricken mother who had lost her daughter through a fluke of nature. She had to blame someone, so she fixed her rage on my father. And when she failed to kill him, she refocused her anger on me."

Jason bent his head to hers, his thumbs stroking her jaw, his fingers warm on her neck. "I never want to go through anything like that again," he murmured. "When I think what might have happened— I love you, Caroline. I think I fell in love with you that night when you were sixteen."

And then there was no more opportunity to talk as his mouth came down over hers in a kiss so sweet and so perfect that Caroline felt it all the way to her toes. Uncaring of the medical personnel who walked past, and of Deputy Black, who rounded the corner and then hastily retreated, Caroline kissed him back with all the love she had in her heart—all the love she'd been holding for him since that long-ago summer night.

15

CAROLINE LAY IN bed at the beach house in Santa Cruz, and listened to the distant crash of the waves against the shore. A week had passed since Marisola Perez had tried to kill her, and she still had a difficult time believing that the nightmare was finally over.

Her father was safe.

She was safe.

Jason had spent most of that day at the courthouse in San Francisco, where her father normally presided, as a different judge listened to preliminary findings on the case. Marisola had spent several days in a psychiatric unit, while doctors determined if she was well enough to stand trial. She'd made her first court appearance that day, and Caroline was grateful that she didn't have to appear. She would, eventually, but not today.

Rolling to her side, she picked up the bedside clock. It was still early, barely nine o'clock, and she knew that Jason was on his way from San Francisco to join her for the weekend.

Now she heard his footsteps on the staircase, and she waited, breathless, as he made his way down the hallway. When he finally pushed the bedroom door open, she sat up.

"Hey," he said, silhouetted against the light in the hallway. "Are you okay?"

"Absolutely okay," she assured him. "Just waiting for you."

She knew he could see her clearly. She wore pale blue baby-doll pajamas with satin straps. The top plunged low in the front and left little to the imagination. Leaving the door ajar, he walked over to the bed, and it wasn't until he stood directly by her side that she could see the smolder in his eyes.

Without taking his eyes from her, he dragged his shirttail out of his waistband and slowly began unfastening the buttons. Peeling the shirt from his body, he fisted his hand in the material of his undershirt and dragged it over his head in one fluid movement.

Caroline's heart lodged in her throat. Shirtless, Jason Cooper was the embodiment of every fantasy she'd ever had. She made no move to touch him when his hands fell to his belt, and he deftly unbuckled it before opening the clasp of his jeans. Slowly, as if he enjoyed tormenting her, he drew his zipper down and then pushed his jeans down the length of his body, toeing his shoes off at the same time, until he stood before her wearing nothing more than his boxer briefs.

"Come here," Caroline whispered and hooked one finger into the waistband of his shorts. She drew him onto the bed, feeling the hot jut of his arousal against the back of her fingers.

He eased himself down on the bed beside her, propping his head on one hand. Reaching out with his free hand, he traced a single finger down her cleavage.

"How was your day?" he asked.

"I couldn't stop thinking about you over at the courthouse and wondering how it was going. What happened?"

"I think Ms. Perez understands just how wrong her actions were," he said quietly. "She's very remorseful."

"Poor woman."

"Don't you feel sorry for her," Jason commanded. "She made her own choices, and she has nobody to blame but herself. Other people have lost children without resorting to attempted murder as a coping mechanism."

"So it's pretty clear that she acted alone?" Caroline asked.

"She enlisted the help of her brother for the break-in here," he said. "It was her brother who disabled the electrical and actually broke in. But she was here, too. For what it's worth, I think her brother was an unwilling accomplice, and I don't think he had any idea of just how far his sister was willing to go to settle the score."

"Wow," Caroline breathed, hardly able to comprehend it all. "So her daughter gets admitted for a routine appendectomy, but nobody knows she has an underlying heart condition. She has a bad reaction to the anesthesia, and dies on the table. They resuscitate her, but she's brain-dead, and after a few days, Marisola has to make the decision to remove her daughter from life support.

Worse, when she files a medical malpractice case, the judge finds on behalf of the hospital."

"Yes."

"So Marisola needs closure. She wants revenge on the person she feels is responsible, and she focuses on my father."

"That's right," Jason said, dipping his head to kiss the soft swell of her breast above the pale blue fabric of her negligee. "But because the judge keeps such late hours, and is hardly ever home, she can't establish a schedule of his activities. She knows if she just sits outside in her car and watches him that people will notice. Like Steven Anderson did that night. But then it seems luck is finally on her side."

As his lips brushed over her sensitive skin, Caroline's fingers curled into the blankets, and she had to struggle to keep her thoughts straight. "My father's neighbor puts out an ad for a housekeeper, and Marisola applies. Now she can watch my father's house. She knows when he's home, and when he's not. Even better, nobody questions her presence in the neighborhood."

"You got it," Jason purred and tugged the fabric down, until her breast sprang free. He devoured her with his eyes. "She blended in. She and her brother did the same thing when they came here. She dressed as a housekeeper, and her brother dressed as the gardener. Nobody thought twice about it or even noticed them."

"Hiding in plain sight," Caroline gasped as Jason dipped his head and drew her dusky nipple into his mouth.

He skated his mouth along the side of her neck and

gently bit her earlobe before soothing the area with his tongue. "She waited for him, hiding in the shrubbery until he came home, and then she simply walked up to his front door and rang the bell."

"He probably didn't even recognize her," Caroline said. "He simply saw a woman in a housekeeping dress, and probably thought she needed help. He was always helping people."

Jason raised his head and looked down at her, his eyes filled with empathy. "Yes. But your father is going to make a full recovery, and Ms. Perez is going to get the help that she needs."

"What a tragedy," Caroline murmured. "I remember reading the case file and thinking that it didn't seem fair for the hospital to get off scot-free. Why did my father rule in their favor?"

Jason made a sympathetic sound. "Without knowing her medical history, there was no way they could have predicted what would happen on the operating table."

Caroline shook her head. "I'm glad she's been caught, but I can't help feeling sorry for her. She lost her daughter."

"And I almost lost you," Jason growled. "Don't feel too sorry for her."

"All this time, we thought it was Eddie Green or Sanchez. But it was a grieving mother."

"You did try to tell me that our most likely bet in finding the shooter was to examine the malpractice cases." He kissed her chin. "Sure you want to become a child welfare advocate? You'd make a great private investigator."

"Hmm." Caroline pretended to consider, winding her

arms around his neck. "My powers of deduction *are* exceptional. Like right now, I know how much you want me."

HE DID WANT HER. He'd spent most of the day thinking about how very differently this whole thing could've gone down, and how close he'd come to losing her. Even before Marisola Perez had attacked Caroline, Jason had decided there was no way in hell he was letting her go. He'd done that once. He wouldn't make the same mistake twice. He'd spent the entire day in court, listening to the preliminary testimony so that the judge could make a ruling on whether or not there would be a trial. When all the facts had been presented, he'd been a little horrified at how close he'd come to losing the two people he cared most about in the whole world.

As he'd driven back to the beach house, knowing that the judge would recover and that Caroline was waiting for him, he'd felt like the luckiest son of a bitch on the face of the planet. He didn't deserve to have so much happiness. He didn't deserve to have his life turn out so freaking good, but he was long past the point where he would question his own good fortune. He'd grab on to it with both hands and be eternally grateful for it.

Now Jason brushed his mouth over Caroline's, their breath mingling as he drew his free hand slowly over her body. "What would cause you to believe that I want you?"

"This," she replied and reached down to cover him with her hand. He was already hard. "And this…"

Leaning into him, she pressed her lips against his in a kiss that made his toes curl. He'd been aroused since he'd opened the bedroom door and spotted her in the bed, looking like a sugary confection in her little blue nightie. He wanted to lick her everywhere.

"God," he muttered against her mouth, "you drive me crazy."

He felt her smile, and he took the opportunity to deepen the kiss and explore the damp silk of her mouth with his tongue. He captured her moan, fusing their lips together as she held his head in her hands.

With supreme effort, he tore his mouth from hers and bit a tender path along her jaw to where her heart pulsed erratically against the base of her throat. She gasped and arched upward, then slid one hand to the small of his back to urge him closer. Bracing his weight on one forearm, he lifted himself away from her enough to grasp the hem of her short nightgown and drag it upward. She helped him, pulling it over her head and tossing it aside until she was gloriously bare beneath him.

"Jesus," he muttered, cupping his hand around one breast. "You're the prettiest thing I've seen all day."

He bent his head and flicked the dusky nipple with his tongue. Her breathing hitched and her hips shifted restlessly beneath him. He stroked the curve of her hip until he encountered the waistband of her silk panties and put his fingers beneath the fabric.

"Take these off," he demanded.

"Yes," she murmured and lifted her hips to help him as he pushed the material down and then she kicked them free.

Jason sucked in his breath at the sight of her pale skin and the shadow of curls at the juncture of her thighs.

Her breasts rose and fell rapidly, and when he stroked the back of his knuckles across her stomach, her muscles contracted.

"I've thought about this all day," he growled.

Two weeks ago, he'd have been scared to death at the intensity of his feelings. Until Caroline had come back into his life, he didn't believe in meaningful relationships. He was committed to his job, and that was it. He'd have run in the opposite direction if any woman had suggested he commit himself to her. But with Caroline, that was all he seemed to want to do. He wanted to commit himself to her—mind, body and soul. He wanted to imprint himself on her so that she would have no doubts that she belonged to him, and that he loved her with every breath he took.

He knew they had some logistical issues to work out, but as far as he was concerned, he'd already won the battle—she wasn't returning to Virginia. Even if she decided to remain in San Francisco, they could make it work. He'd been making the trip from San Diego about every month in order to see her father. He figured he could do it every weekend, if he needed to. Or he could fly her down to stay with him.

Right now, with her sprawled beneath him, his own arousal was such that he pushed his own misgivings about their future aside. He wanted her.

Badly.

She still cupped him through his briefs, and the sensation of her hand on his rigid cock caused him to groan. He bent his head once more and caught her mouth with his own. She responded by arching against him and sliding her lips against his so that pleasure lashed through him. She stroked him through the fabric of his boxers, before easing her hand beneath the waistband to grasp him in her fingers. Her touch was like an electric shock, and he quivered reflexively in her hand.

"You're so hard," she murmured against his mouth, stroking one finger across the head of his erection, "and hot."

Oh, yeah.

He eased himself to his side to give her better access to his body, holding her in the curve of his arm as he used his free hand to explore her more fully. She turned into him, and he ran his hand along the curve of her waist and over her hip before cupping her buttock, enjoying the satiny softness of her skin. But when he dipped his fingers between her cheeks and stroked her intimately from behind, she gave a cry of surprise and jerked against him.

"Shh," he soothed, stroking her. "Let me."

She made an incoherent sound and pressed damp kisses against his throat, even as her hand continued to explore him. He was stiff and aching and wanted nothing more than to turn her onto her back, spread her thighs and thrust himself into her, but he forced himself to slow down. He separated her feminine folds with his fingers.

"Ah, sweetheart," he said. "You're already wet." Slowly, he eased one finger into her, feeling her inner muscles contract around him even as she closed her hand around his cock. She was incredibly tight, and his balls ached with the need for release.

She withdrew her hand from his body and wordlessly pushed his boxers down until he could shimmy them free. Then there was nothing between them.

Jason hooked a hand behind her knee and drew her leg across his hip, opening her for him as he resumed stroking her and swirling moisture over the small rise of flesh until she made an inarticulate sound of pleasure and shivered in his arms.

"Good?" he murmured against her ear before tracing the delicate lobe with his tongue.

"Oh, yes," she said. "So good."

Easing two fingers into her, he thrust them slowly in and out, and then caught her mouth with his own, using his tongue to imitate the movement of his hand. She moaned deeply.

Pushing her onto her back, Jason came over her and began working his way down the length of her body with his mouth while continuing to torment her with his fingers. She watched him through hazy eyes, her lower lip caught between her teeth. He licked her breasts, suckling first one nipple and then the other before moving lower, skating his tongue along her smooth stomach while his fingers worked strongly inside her. Her hips lifted into his hand, and when he reached her navel, he dipped his tongue inside before trailing his lips lower, to kiss the inside of one thigh. Then, as he continued to stroke her, he bent his head and touched his tongue to her clitoris. She gave a strangled cry and her hips bucked, but Jason had no mercy. He continued to lave her with gentle laps, while his fingers caressed her until she cried out and her whole body convulsed. He felt her muscles contracting around his fingers, but he didn't stop until he'd wrung every last shiver from her and she collapsed weakly against the pillow.

Only then did he come fully over her, using his knee to spread her thighs. He was completely jacked, but he still had enough sense to reach over and jerk open the drawer of the bedside table and pull out an unopened box of condoms. Watching her come apart had been a total turn-on. With hands that weren't quite steady, he ripped the box open and peeled a condom from a foil packet.

"Okay?" he asked, husky with desire.

She gave a shaky laugh and drew him down. "I don't know," she confessed. "Am I still alive?"

"Oh, yeah," he said and covered himself. "Let me show you."

IT SEEMED LIKE hours later when Caroline lay sprawled over Jason's chest, her breasts flattened against his skin as she gazed at him and ran one finger along the seam of his lips.

"How do you do it?" she marveled.

He lay back against the pillows, one arm bent behind his head as he leisurely stroked her hair. "Do what?"

"Make each time with you even better than the last."

He grinned. "I thought that was you."

Caroline rested her cheek against his chest and let her fingers trace lazy patterns around the flat nub of his nipple.

"So what happens now?" she asked.

He dragged in a deep sigh. "Well, we caught the shooter, so you and your father are safe. We've pulled his protection detail off the assignment. He no longer needs the services of the U.S. Marshals."

She didn't look at him. "So I guess the same goes for

me, too. I expect you're ready to get back to San Diego and pick up the reins again."

"I expect so."

She raised her head and stared at him in the dim light. "Really?"

He shrugged. "There's no reason for me to stay here any longer, Caroline. I came to protect you, and now you no longer need that protection. What would you have me do? My job here is done."

"Is it?" she mused.

"Why don't you tell me?" he suggested.

Caroline inched herself up his body, until she could straddle his hips and frame his face in both of her hands. Jason swallowed convulsively, and she didn't miss how his eyes dropped to her breasts, or how he shifted restlessly beneath her.

"Jason Cooper," she began, "I've wanted you for as long as I can remember. From the time you were nothing more than a skinny boy with a bad attitude." She leaned down to kiss him. "I wanted you when I was sixteen and just learning what it was like to be a woman. And now that you've shown me how wonderful that is, I don't want to be with anyone else."

"Caroline—"

"I trusted you with my body. I trusted you with my life." She smiled down at him. "And you're the only man I'll ever trust with my heart."

He made a sound of protest, and Caroline laid two fingers over his mouth. "So you see, I'm going to need you around for a very long time, because all three of those are now yours to keep and to protect."

Reaching up, Jason caught her fingers in his hand and turned his mouth into her palm, kissing her reverently. When he looked at her, the emotion reflected in his eyes was enough to stop her breath.

"Caroline Banks," he said, his voice low and a little rough. "It looks like you've got yourself a deal. But I have to warn you that I take my job seriously. I'm going to be around for a very long time."

With a sigh of relief, Caroline lowered her mouth to his. "I definitely like the sound of that, Marshal Cooper."

And then no more words were spoken, and the only sound was that of the distant surf as it pounded the beach.

* * * * *

COMING NEXT MONTH FROM

HARLEQUIN® *Blaze*®

Available May 20, 2014

#799 RIDING HIGH
Sons of Chance • by Vicki Lewis Thompson

Free-spirited Lily King is in over her head at her new horse sanctuary. Thankfully hunky horse vet Regan O'Connelli is on loan from the Last Chance. Regan is healing a broken heart, and Lily doesn't just want to be a rebound—but neither can resist the temptation....

#800 TESTING THE LIMITS
Uniformly Hot! • by Kira Sinclair

Quinn Keller's been trying to keep her distance from army ranger Jace Hyland—her ex-fiancé's brother—since the day she met him, but now that her life's in danger he's exactly the man she needs.

#801 NEED YOU NOW
Made in Montana • by Debbi Rawlins

Good girl and preacher's daughter Melanie Knowles has lived a sheltered life in Blackfoot Falls, Montana. No one could ever imagine she has a secret thing for bad boys...that is until ex-con Lucas Sloan comes to town.

#802 FINAL SCORE
Last Bachelor Standing • by Nancy Warren

Firefighter Dylan Cross, aka Mr. June in the annual "hottie" calendar, is used to risking his life to save others. But he's not about to risk his heart—or his bachelorhood!—when it comes to sexy Cassie Price....

HBCNM0514

REQUEST YOUR FREE BOOKS!
2 FREE NOVELS PLUS 2 FREE GIFTS!

HARLEQUIN®

Blaze®

red-hot reads!

YES! Please send me 2 FREE Harlequin® Blaze™ novels and my 2 FREE gifts (gifts are worth about $10). After receiving them, if I don't wish to receive any more books, I can return the shipping statement marked "cancel." If I don't cancel, I will receive 4 brand-new novels every month and be billed just $4.74 per book in the U.S. or $4.96 per book in Canada. That's a savings of at least 14% off the cover price. It's quite a bargain. Shipping and handling is just 50¢ per book in the U.S. and 75¢ per book in Canada.* I understand that accepting the 2 free books and gifts places me under no obligation to buy anything. I can always return a shipment and cancel at any time. Even if I never buy another book, the two free books and gifts are mine to keep forever.

150/350 HDN F4WC

Name	(PLEASE PRINT)

Address	Apt. #

City	State/Prov.	Zip/Postal Code

Signature (if under 18, a parent or guardian must sign)

Mail to the **Harlequin® Reader Service**:
IN U.S.A.: P.O. Box 1867, Buffalo, NY 14240-1867
IN CANADA: P.O. Box 609, Fort Erie, Ontario L2A 5X3

Want to try two free books from another line?
Call 1-800-873-8635 or visit www.ReaderService.com.

* Terms and prices subject to change without notice. Prices do not include applicable taxes. Sales tax applicable in N.Y. Canadian residents will be charged applicable taxes. Offer not valid in Quebec. This offer is limited to one order per household. Not valid for current subscribers to Harlequin Blaze books. All orders subject to credit approval. Credit or debit balances in a customer's account(s) may be offset by any other outstanding balance owed by or to the customer. Please allow 4 to 6 weeks for delivery. Offer available while quantities last.

Your Privacy—The Harlequin® Reader Service is committed to protecting your privacy. Our Privacy Policy is available online at www.ReaderService.com or upon request from the Harlequin Reader Service.

We make a portion of our mailing list available to reputable third parties that offer products we believe may interest you. If you prefer that we not exchange your name with third parties, or if you wish to clarify or modify your communication preferences, please visit us at www.ReaderService.com/consumerschoice or write to us at Harlequin Reader Service Preference Service, P.O. Box 9062, Buffalo, NY 14269. Include your complete name and address.

HB13R2

SPECIAL EXCERPT FROM

HARLEQUIN Blaze®

New York Times bestselling author
Vicki Lewis Thompson is back with three new
sizzling titles from her bestselling miniseries
Sons of Chance.

Riding High

"Caution. Proceeding with it."

"You want to proceed?"

"I do." Her eyes darkened to midnight-blue and her gentle sigh was filled to the brim with surrender as her arms slid around his neck, depositing mud along the way.

As if he gave a damn. His body hummed with anticipation. "Me, too." Slowly he lowered his head and closed his eyes.

"Mistake, though."

He hovered near her mouth, hardly daring to breathe. Had she changed her mind at the last minute? "Why?"

"Tell you later." She brought his head down and made the connection.

And it was as electric as he'd imagined. His blood fizzed as it raced through his body and eventually settled in his groin. Her lips fit perfectly against his from the first moment of contact. It seemed his mouth had been created for kissing Lily, and vice versa.

He tried a different angle, just to test that theory. Still perfect, still high-voltage. Since they were standing in water, it was a wonder they didn't short out. He couldn't speak for her but he'd bet he was glowing. His skin was hot enough to send off sparks.

She moaned and pressed her body closer. She felt amazing in his arms—soft, wet and slippery. He'd never imagined doing it in the mud, but suddenly that seemed like the best idea in the world.

Then she snorted. Odd. Not the reaction he would have expected considering where this seemed to be heading.

He lifted his head and gazed into her flushed face. "Did you just laugh?"

She regarded him with passion-filled eyes. "That wasn't me."

"Then who—"

The snort came again as something bumped the back of his knees. A heavy splash sent water up the back of his legs.

She might not have been laughing before but she was now. "Um, we have company."

Although it didn't matter which pig had interrupted the moment, Regan had his money on Harley. Whichever one had decided to take an after-dinner mud bath, they'd ruined what had been a very promising kiss.

Pick up RIDING HIGH by Vicki Lewis Thompson, available June 2014 wherever Harlequin® Blaze® books are sold!

And don't miss RIDING HARD and RIDING HOME in July and August of 2014!

It feels good to be bad!

Good girl and preacher's daughter Melanie Knowles has lived a sheltered life in Blackfoot Falls, Montana. No one could ever imagine she has a secret thing for bad boys... that is until ex-con Lucas Sloan comes to town.

Don't miss the latest in the
Made in Montana miniseries

Need You Now
by reader-favorite author
Debbi Rawlins

Available June 2014 wherever you buy
Harlequin Blaze books.